MURDER IN THE OBSERVATION CAR

The Railway Mystery Series

Book One

www.instagram.com/railwaymysteries

MURDER IN THE OBSERVATION CAR

BEN H. MORRISON

INTERLOCKING PRESS

First paperback edition November 2019

ISBN 978-1-7340356-1-2

Published by Interlocking Press

www.interlockingpress.com

PROLOGUE

December 1946

CINCINNATI UNION TERMINAL

The fourth try successfully ignited the tobacco. Merciless, the winter wind sliced through his overcoat as the man who could hardly remember the name he travelled under suppressed a shiver.

Snapping shut the lighter, he greedily inhaled the warmth of the cigarette, the blaze at its tip momentarily adding to the dim, pale lights of the platform. The massive dome of the Union Terminal stood sphinxlike in the distance, concealing beneath it the petty dramas of a thousand travelers rushing to find their trains. Its concourse stretched over the tracks for what seemed like miles, its dozens of staircases branching off like the legs of a massive arachnid, guiding passengers to platforms below just like his own.

Visible before him between gaps in the freight and passenger trains standing in the rail yard, the dark outline of a departing train glided steadily by. The yellow lights of the windows flickered with the movement of silhouettes, indistinct figures sliding in and out of view as the train continued its journey. The dull-sharp *thud-THUD thud-THUD* of the wheels on the joints of the rail echoed regularly, lending the scene a mechanistic eternality, stable and predictable and comforting.

The machine that was the yard thudded on and on, taking no notice of the man and caring not at all about his mission. The final car came into view—an observation car, a social space outfitted with extra-large windows and a lounge in which to gather. As he watched the silhouettes sharing boisterous laughter and exchanging stolen glances, drinking and reading and storytelling, he allowed himself a rare philosophical moment.

"A window to America. That is the train," he said softly to himself in a voice deep and grave that betrayed no hint of accent nor dialect nor origin. "For me, at least." Subconsciously, he fingered the outline of the pistol against his ribcage.

THUD-THUD thud-THUD thud-THUD thud-THUD thud-thud replied the yard.

He flicked his cigarette to the ground as the conductor called from further up the platform, "The *Union* for Roanoke, Lynchburg, and Norfolk! All aboard!"

The shrillness of the whistle that followed pierced the man as brutally as the wind. It was time to go. He cast a last glance down the platform at the train. A black beast of a steam locomotive stood at its head, its streamlined shroud giving it the appearance of a bullet poised in mid-flight. Behind it stood a collection of burgundy baggage cars and coaches lettered in gold NORFOLK & WESTERN RAILWAY, the carrier that would haul the train on the next leg of its journey from Chicago to the east. Last in line were the green Pullman sleeping cars, the first-class hotels- and clubs-on-wheels that carried those with the distance to require and the means to afford them. The flurries had gathered, giving each black-roofed car a dusting of pure white.

He hoisted himself back onto his carriage where the porter waited to take his coat and hat. It was late, and a glance down the corridor revealed that most of the ten passenger sections had already been made up into sleeping berths for night. The

Christmas traffic ensured that nearly all of the twenty available beds had been engaged.

The porter sensed what he was thinking, "Turning in for the night, sir?"

A perfunctory reply, weary: "No, I have work to do." He started down the corridor for the small lounge at the far end of his carriage.

The porter spared only a moment's thought at the strangeness of the man heading to a crowded and lively lounge to do work at 10:30 on a Sunday night. He, too, had forgotten the man's name, and even the recollection of his face was rapidly fading. Had he known, the man might have approved and taken it as a complement to his craft, but the black porter was beneath his contemplation in any case. A buzzer down the corridor drew the porter away, and the two men were mutually forgotten.

The train pulled out of the station and plunged into the night.

CHAPTER ONE

January 1948

RMS QUEEN MARY

Not for the first time, James Brummell silently cursed water, oceans, ships, people who build ships, and his masters at the State Department who wrongheadedly insisted that American diplomacy required the presence of diplomats overseas.

The dining room of the great ocean liner again bucked beneath him—or, at least, it *seemed* to buck even as the fine bone china and the glistening silverware somehow sat unmoving on the table. His eyes—and his reason—told James he was merely seasick. His stomach told him the world was shortly to end.

Given his circumstances, he silently wondered if that might not be so bad after all. Upon his boyish—some might even say, babyish—face, already pale from the cold and dreary last few months, was plastered an obviously false half-smile at which any observant conversant would have taken alarm. His lunch companion, a doughty and stalwart figure of a matriarch who assured James that she occupied a place at the summit of St. Louis society, was not such a person. She droned on. And on.

"And, as I told my husband time and again, there is simply *no substitute* for American ingenuity. Why, look at the English countryside—it's like stepping back into the Dark Ages!"

It is said that the walls between passengers gradually crumble by the fourth day of a sea voyage. Unable to rebuild them even using his newly-green complexion as a magnet for sympathy, James braced for yet another of the lady's unsolicited lectures on the evils of European society. His stomach kicked again—as much from surprise as nausea—when she instead ceased fire: "But of course, I'm sure that a bright young man like you can see these things for yourself. What work did you say you do?"

"I didn't, actually," he replied, covering the bite in his tone with a wider, even more insincere smile. "I work for the State Department. I've been in Europe, mainly France, for the past six months."

"Oh, a *diplomat*!" she exclaimed, pregnant with meaning. As she started down yet another conversational cul-de-sac, James refocused his attention on the horizon provided by the deck, his eyes narrowing slightly as he reminded himself that he was a human being planted firmly and safely on a great ship, a great ship floating confidently upon the ocean, an ocean clinging calmly and majestically to the—

Something in her monologue snapped James out of his reverie: "So *you're* one of the fellows giving our money away to these foreigners? That George Marshall plan? Seems an *awful* waste to me—they'll just spend it and ask for more! Of course, they could use a bit of guidance from America—businesslike, that's our method. Giving away our money, though—"

"Yes, m'am," he gently interrupted, preparing for a conversation he anticipated repeating often in the near future. His stomach momentarily forgotten, he began an answer he had been carefully developing by trial-and-error since the voyage began. A large, well-built man with a physique that suggested more muscle than he actually possessed, James straightened himself slightly, tugged on the vest—*waistcoat*, as they said on Saville Row—he wore underneath his jacket, and continued.

"I *am* a diplomat, though not a very important one, and I do indeed work on the European Recovery Project, which everybody calls the Marshall Plan." He inhaled slightly and leaned in, as though taking her into his confidence, "You're right, of course, that the Secretary of State's program of loans and gifts to our friends in Europe is risky," he paused for effect, "but *all* investments carry risk, and this is an investment that we must make."

She drew back, "What do you mean, investment? Why, my husband invests all the time and he—"

"Well, m'am," he again cut in, "you see, the communists in the Soviet Union are hoping that the economies of our European friends will fail and that they will begin to despair. That will allow the Reds to more easily take control of our friends. If we're to stop that from happening—and, I'm sure you yourself are a firm opponent of communism..."

"Oh, yes! Horrid ideas! Horrid people! The papers say the communists will make us all farm beets and take all of our—."

"Precisely. So if we want to stop that from happening, we have to invest *now* in Europe. Help them get their economies back on their feet, get them producing again and trading with us for all of our wonderful goods."

Sensing from the blank look on her face that the conversation was overly abstract, James cast about for a detail to drive home his point. He was good at details, good at focusing in on things that mattered in the moment and using them to his advantage. His eyes darted up and down his companion as though seeing her for the first time. Middle-aged, plumping considerably, overly rouged, clearly middle class but with pretens—

There. He saw it, a pair of gloves fringed in a fine lace, probably Belgian. They would do.

"Take those gloves you're wearing. I gather you bought them

in northern France, maybe Belgium?"

"Why, yes, my husband took me to Lille and I found them in a shop there—it was an absurd sum! But such fine stitch-work…" She straightened her arm and spread her hand, admiring them.

"Yes, precisely," he replied in a soothing tone. "You see, that fine Belgian lace you have on them—so flattering, if you don't mind me saying…"

"Not at all," she replied warmly.

"You see, it's so expensive because the war wrecked the Belgian and French economies. There's not enough coal to provide enough light, for example, to allow the workers to work full days. It's so much harder to make good gloves in any quantity under such circumstances. Shoot, sometimes there's not even enough food because the city-folk don't have anything to trade to the farmers for their produce. Factories have been flattened, and so many men killed and women and children displaced—are you a mother?"

"Yes, of two wonderful boys. They're with their aunt, but I couldn't help but think of them when I saw these emaciated little urchins in the streets of Paris. So sad!"

"Indeed, indeed." He paused for effect. "If France and Belgium and all our other friends in Europe are going to be able to get back on their feet and feed those children and make those gloves, they need capital to invest in rebuilding their power plants and factories and roads and all the other things needed to make goods. Then, they'll bring them to market for honest Americans like yourself to buy and import. In exchange, we'll pay them with corn and grain and all the products of our own industry and, of course, our dollars, which have become the most important currency in the world. We'll grow more prosperous and influential by helping our friends trade and prosper themselves."

He sat back slightly and quickly sipped water from the glass in front of him. He hoped the movement disguised the small beads of sweat that had appeared on his brow.

Somewhat dazzled, she asked with a hint of skepticism, "Will it really work?"

He leaned forward once more, and fixed her with his most sincere gaze. "With the support of the American people, yes," he replied.

"Genuinely?"

"Absolutely."

"*We* can really fix this?" For a moment, her earlier chauvinism was forgotten, and in its place stood what James clearly perceived to be a frightened, deeply-felt but never-spoken-of insecurity about the future. *Almost child-like*, James thought to himself. *Just like America itself, a child with the world suddenly thrust upon it.* He held her gaze.

"I'm sure of it."

He had her, now the *coup de grâce*. "And, along the way, we'll build a better, more prosperous world that will be extremely advantageous to our own business. And we'll keep those Soviets where they belong, far away from our shores."

Business, like a charmed incantation, cinched it for the lady, and the invocation of the Soviet threat was the cherry on top. The brief glimpse behind the curtain was gone, and she was again herself—*or at least the self she wishes me to see*, thought James.

"Well, that puts a different color on it entirely! I'll have to write to my husband and see what he thinks about this—it's certainly a different point of view than I've heard before! That General Marshall should have you do his talking for him, you're such a nice young man with such a wonderful way with words!" And again she was off.

James did not confirm for her that he was traveling back to the United States to do effectively just that. His next posting for the State Department was a speaking tour of civic organizations around the country to explain—and, hopefully, bring people around to—the Marshall Plan for aid to Europe. Indeed, he would begin this enterprise in less than a week, allowing time only for a stopover in Washington to consult with his superiors. His tickets west for the following evening had already been booked and waited on him at the capital's Union Station. Instead, he remained silent and endured her effusive compliments with the same patient grace a soldier endures a friendly bombardment landing just a little too close to his foxhole.

As though in response, his stomach rumbled deeply, making him momentarily wistful for any dry land—even the battlefront he had seen briefly during the war—and more than a little concerned for the integrity of the club sandwich he had just consumed. He focused on the silver spoon sitting before him, the CUNARD name proudly advertising the line upon which he sailed. The engraving was solid and new upon the spoon, and he fixated upon it as he tried to recover his balance.

The moment he again felt seaworthy—and his new good friend paused for breath—James made his excuses and retreated to his stateroom.

Leaning over his sink, he let the water flow. A bracing splash of cold water to his face calmed him as he appraised himself in the mirror. His twenty-nine years wore less heavily on him than they might have. He still had a full head of soft, thick, if somewhat wispy brown hair. His brown eyes had developed their first crow's feet in the course of his work the past few months. Though bags protruded from beneath them more often than not, they still had a youthful quality—a hopefulness and expressiveness about them—that fooled most casual observers. He could pass for younger than he really was, especially when clean shaven.

He sank down onto his bed as he contemplated the task before him. A great deal of travel, a great many faces and places to meet and abandon in the coming months. He resolved to rest while he could, and to enjoy as much leisure as possible on the many legs of travel to the Midwest that stood before him. There would not be much time before he was back in the thick of things.

He laid down for a nap, figuring it best to grab every second of sleep. Only a few more hours to New York.

CHAPTER TWO

NEW YORK CITY

Disembarking from a great ocean liner is like any other international travel experience: packing light and carrying a diplomatic passport tend to speed the process along. Well-equipped on both fronts, James had no problem making his way off the ship and into the maritime terminal on the far western shore of Manhattan Island. He paused as stepped onto *terra firma*, taking in the dusk scene around him.

He had always loved transportation hubs—the rush of people heading in every direction, the thrill of puzzling out where they had come from and where they were going. As a boy, he would urge his parents to reach train and ferry stations early, just so he could look at the luggage being hauled about by the porters. The stickers and tags those pieces carried were like little clues to the meaning of life, gateways to distant shores and windows onto the lives of all peoples.

The great and the good. The famous, the infamous, and the obscure, James thought as he watched a newsboy in a ragged flat hat sell a paper first to a longshoreman fresh from the dock and then turn around and sell the same paper to a man James vaguely recognized as a minor British noble, immaculately clad in silks.

All of it here, laid before me like a scene in a play. Or a puzzle.

Gathering himself, James solicited a paper from the newsboy and set off for the cab queue. Securing a taxi was also no challenge, and he was grateful given the storm clouds he could make out in the moonlight gathering across the Hudson River. His luggage secure in the trunk, he flopped into the cab and tossed his hat onto the seat beside him. "Pennsylvania Station, please," he told the driver.

As the cab entered traffic, James cast his eyes away from the newspaper he had bought, now sitting limply in his lap. He instead contemplated the thunderheads as the cab sped him a dozen blocks south the station, trying all the while to avoid drawing the obvious analogy between the coming storm and the front-page headline that stared up at him: SOVIETS MAKE THREATS OVER BERLIN.

The cab turned down 34th Street and James scrutinized the station. It was less a building than a monument; one of the largest single spaces under one roof anywhere in the world, it spanned several city blocks. Its classical façade of massive columns elevated the eye to the glorious pediments crowning the scene. This temple of transportation—and, indeed, of the American Republic itself—beckoned millions each year to ride the fast, modern trains of the stately Pennsylvania Railroad, proudly billed as 'The Standard Railroad of the World'.

Shifting in his seat as the cab rounded a curve, James spared a moment's thought for the unseen, but even more important, pair of tunnels running under the Hudson that brought trains to and from the mainland. The Pennsylvania had built those tunnels itself, an enormous risk that paid off despite widespread naysaying at the time. Competitor railroads still terminated their trains in Jersey City and ferried their customers across over the water; Pennsylvania passengers simply glided underneath the water thanks to those miracles of modern engineering.

Deposited at the underground cab queue, he rested his two suitcases at the station's threshold and pulled his pocket watch from his waistcoat. James preferred the three-piece suit that he now wore to the fashionable two-piece more commonly seen; the addition of the vest allowed him places for a watch in the left pocket along with the travel ephemera and bric-a-brac he routinely collected while in motion in the right. Both the watch and the suit were slightly behind the times, but James preferred the steady stateliness of both elements, formerly staples of menswear for a century. *Traditions should be preserved*, he thought, *traditions of professionalism and taste and sophistication.* That he also thought they flattered his broad frame was beside the point, or so he told himself.

The watch told him it was already after 7:45. Having consulted a railway guide on the *Queen Mary*, he knew it was too late to make the 7:55 departure of the Pennsylvania Railroad's *Patriot* toward Washington. He would have to settle for the next train offered, the 8:30 *Constitution.* If he hurried, he might be able to get a first-class seat in the parlor car. Replacing the watch, he hefted his luggage and started inside.

No matter how many times he had passed through the grand entrance hall, the view remained awe-inspiring. The gods themselves would have felt at home here. Marble walls stretched up toward ceilings in the sky, decorative octagons adorning the massive vaulting at their summit. Beyond, toward the trains, pillars of decorative metal branched up to support a ceiling of glass. Sunlight burst down into the space, lighting the way to the stairs heading down toward the platforms beneath the station. But, most of all, the *people.* Endless, numberless hordes of them. All promenading through this titanic space, all about the important business of moving themselves from where they were to where they wished to be.

Stirring himself from his reverie, James maneuvered his bulk through the crowd and to the ticket window. "Good evening. A parlor car seat for the 8:30 to Washington, if you have the space."

"Certainly sir, one moment and I'll check," the clerk replied.

A phone call downstairs to the warren where thousands of train seats and berths were tracked confirmed the availability, and the clerk issued James two tickets, one for the Pennsylvania, which would haul the train, and the other for a seat in one of the Pullman-operated parlor cars. After months of travel on war-torn European railways—to say nothing of his harrowing experience on board ship—he looked forward to the comfort of a Pullman. Taking his tickets, he scrutinized the one issued by the Pullman Company; it was color-coded to reference the type of accommodation purchased, and this one was the correct green color indicating a private parlor seat for the four hour ride into Washington.

Taking his tickets, James hurried from the window to the Great Hall as an announcement rang out, "Now boarding train 147, the *Constitution*, for Philadelphia and Washington. All aboard. All aboard, track 9." He felt his pace quicken as the promises of a seat, a drink, a meal, and a quick run over his last leg of transit for the day all lured him forward.

Descending the stairs to the platforms below, he encountered a dozen or so carriages, must of them coaches painted in varying shades of faded Tuscan red. Two were colored differently, the forest-dark shade known as Pullman green that signaled the car carried first-class accommodations and was owned by Pullman itself in the 'pool' of such cars regularly rotating around the country according to demand. He headed toward them slowly, finding that his desire to admire the steel beast momentarily overwhelmed his other demands.

James found his own car—gold letters on its side informing him it was christened *Mask and Wig Club* after what he vaguely remembered was a fraternity of some sort at the University of Pennsylvania—at the very back of the train. He paused, touching its cold steel side. James reflected briefly on the untold miles it had likely travelled and places it had seen.

A white-jacketed man with black skin, the porter, stepped down from the carriage.

"Hello, sir, are you one of my passengers this evenin'?"

"I am indeed. Seat 8."

"Let me help you with that luggage." He suited action to words by taking his cases on board. James followed.

"And what are you called, porter?" James asked as his bags were being stowed. He knew Pullman porters were commonly called 'George' in the same manner, contemptuous or affectionate, that Americans belted out '*garçon*!' at the cafes of Paris. It was an absurdly discourteous practice, and the almost obsessive focus on courtesy with which James had been brought up rebelled against it.

"George, sir. George Hunter," the porter said with a smile.

Deflated, James covered politely, "Well, I'm called James. James Brummell. Pleasure."

It was only then James realized he was letting some of his French slip through. One does not 'call oneself' something in the United States, one simply *is*. He'd have to adjust back to normal quickly if he was to become 'a diplomat to our own people', as his superiors had put it. He suddenly felt very tired.

George led him to his seat, one of a dozen swiveling arm chairs. He sank down into its plush burgundy grasp and surveyed his surroundings. The car was decorated to evoke a men's club of London or New York. The parlor seating area was built for each of its occupants to comfortably read a newspaper, use the small table provided to write, or to simply gaze out the window at the passing scenery, contemplating stocks or bonds or whatever wealthy, northeastern men of means think about. The subdued atmosphere in the parlor area clearly discouraged conversing, so a separate kitchen, dining area, and drinks lounge lay beyond a glass partition halfway down the car.

Remembering the newspaper he had kept with him, he halfheartedly unfolded it. Again, the ominous headline stared back at him. The Russians were making moves toward the little enclave of West Berlin. There, a small contingent of American, British, and French troops guarded half of a city while surrounded by Soviet-occupied territory. This arrangement had seemed safe when the wartime allies were on good terms. Now that the Iron Curtain, as Churchill had put it over a year ago, had descended, that little enclave was in danger of being swallowed up. James had just left Europe, but the troubles of Europe refused to leave him.

Thinking about it, he found himself exhaling, almost sighing, audibly. He added a frown: James disliked it when his internal monologue escaped into the wild.

Only the slightest of jolts signaled the train had departed. An old, all-steel heavyweight like the *Mask and Wig Club* was expert at insulating its riders from the jars and bumps of the switches the train passed through as it pulled out of the station. The gentle rocking motion as the carriage traversed the joints of the rail and the points of the switches gave the experience a nautical feel; unlike a real sea voyage, however, this motion comforted James rather than nauseating him.

A greedy eater since youth, his mind soon turned to his next meal. Eager to have a bite before it got too busy, James waited what he calculated to be a socially-acceptable amount of time after the conductors checked his tickets to bolt for the lounge. The ill-omened newspaper came with him.

Outside, a burst of air pressure signaled that the train had exited the tunnel under the Hudson River and entered New Jersey. As he entered the dining area, James glanced out the window, his attention drawn by flashes of lightning across the bogs and marshes of the area. It was as though God had scoured the area of anything save tall grasses; only occasional rail lines and industrial plants interrupted the primordial feeling of the scene.

Inside, the situation was more civilized. The dining area in front of him was fashionably decorated with painted glass partitions, crisply-laid place settings, and fine linens. Beyond it, a lounge area meant for cocktails and conversation beckoned. A few figures, all male, had beaten even James there.

The attendant greeted him, "Welcome, sir. Would you like a table?"

"A drink in the lounge first, I think. A Gibson. With Plymouth." James replied.

Passing through the dinette, he seated himself on a small couch facing inward toward the isle. Next to him was a fat man with glasses whose brave remnant of wispy white hair was fighting a rearguard action against the forces of time. James made out from the corner of his eye a cheap blue suit in pinstripes that seemed somewhat bold—a critic would say, *loud*—and out of place.

Directly across from him was a nondescript man in a grey suit. Unlike James's tailored three-piece, the man's grey suit was a more popular double-breasted cut worn without a vest. Also unlike James, his fabric was of clearly coarser quality—fabric of the type worn by travelers or others whose business clothes were roughly treated.

James turned to his newspaper once more as his the waiter arrived and mixed his Gibson martini. The ritual was carried out with precision: the liquor and mixer offered for inspection, and then mixed in sight of the customer. Taking the cool cocktail glass in hand, James sipped it slowly, savoring the flavor of the onion garnish and the earthy, sweet taste of the Plymouth gin. His other hand held the paper as he skimmed the depressing details of the situation in Germany. The train rocked slightly as it bounced through a switch at high speed.

"You really follow that stuff?" said the man beside him with a quick, hurried voice. It seemed as though the man's bulk weighed heavily upon him. A few beads of sweat on his forehead confirmed this.

"Yes, I'm afraid I do." James replied, looking up with a tolerant smile. "Have to for work." He tried not to flinch as another lightning strike in the distance underscored his words.

"Well, young man, you can tell me what that Stalin is playin' at. He's playin' at *somethin'* though, idn'tee?" James was unsure whether the wheezing was at fault for the accent or if it was native to some as-yet-undiscovered American region.

"Oh yes," he began his reply, "the Russians have no shortage of tricks, games, and riddles when it comes to Europe." Hearing his own words, James inwardly chastised himself for the fatigue and frustration he knew he had let slip through.

A voice intruded, smooth and confident. "You sound as though you speak from experience."

It was the man across from him. James studied him for a moment before responding. His hair was dark, almost black, with just a slight hint of grey. His face was dreadfully bland, with cheekbones, lips, eyes, and brow all seemingly calculated to be utterly median and undistinctive. The smoothness of his voice and the ease of his manner belied the utter forgettability of his appearance.

Salesman, James thought, *about 39 or 40*. The man's unusually large wristwatch caught the corner of his eye. *Moderately prosperous. Perhaps Bibles. Dry goods.* His eyes darted upward as a bemused smile appeared on the man's face, a look inviting shared confidence or jocularity. Something about that smile linked with the dark brown eyes inches above to draw James in. He revised upward his estimation of the man's prosperity. *A* true *salesman, perhaps*, James amended.

Only a split second had passed. James was good at this. "Yes, you're actually right. I've just returned from Europe. I work for the State Department." James paused, awaiting the questions he knew he would be fielding for the next several months.

The fat man adjacent sputtered, "You mean you wak in Wassington?"

"I do. Well, actually, I'm on my way out west to take care of some business there. So, Chicago, Milwaukee, and Seattle, among others, will be my station for a few months."

"This *ain't* the train to Chicago, ya know," came the pointed reply.

"Yes, I'm just laying over in Washington tonight," James parried. "Tomorrow, I'll stop by my department and then catch the evening train to St. Louis. That's my first engagement."

"What work you do for the *State Department* in *St. Louis*?" the man asked, again with a hint of challenge in his voice.

"Publicity work, mostly. I talk to citizens' groups about what's happening in Europe and how the aid we're sending over there works."

Redness entered the fat man's face as he began a thorough disquisition on the evils of foreign aid. The words came so fast they began to carry with them spittle.

Sensing the direction events were taking, the man in the grey suit excused himself with a "good evening" spoken in low tones. As he stood, he cast his gaze directly at James, his dark brown eyes suddenly taking on a sympathetic air as the corners of his mouth bent just slightly upward. It was an efficient gesture, only a split second in the making, yet it briefly unified the two men in shared agony at the prospect of conversation with a third. And then he was gone.

Oh yes, a true *salesman indeed*, James thought.

The fat man's head of steam seemed to be reducing as he circled the problem of whether it was more un-American to *want* to fight the Russians or to *not* want to fight the Russians. James struggled to keep a sympathetic look on his face as the image of a fat spaniel chasing its tail came to mind. Glancing up and away from the fat man to stifle the temptation to laugh, he saw the departing man in grey speak to the waiter; a moment later he was seated at his own table in the dinette.

Ten minutes had passed before James was able to pry himself from the conversation of his corpulent companion, having at last convinced him of the basic rationality of American policy in Europe. Under normal circumstances, he would have considered this a triumph. Presently, his cocktail glass was as empty as his stomach, and he could think only of food. He rose, swaying slightly as the train raced along at speed, and entered the dinette.

The attendant greeted him. "Sir, may I possibly seat you with another guest? We are expecting to be full up momentarily."

This was a standard practice on many railroads and, though James was not particularly fond of it, he conceded with good grace, "Yes, certainly."

Stepping backwards, the attendant seated him at the same table that the man in the grey suit had occupied only minutes before. An awkward moment ensued—that first moment, when seated with a stranger, in which both parties silently size each other up. Who would speak first (or at all)? What topics would be appropriate, what connections might be shared?

James paused, looking out the window but seeing only the reflection of the two men at the table. The blackness beyond had combined with the light in the car to transform the glass into a hazy, slightly twisted mirror image of the gazer. Attempting to look outside, to escape the train and the momentary awkwardness of the table proved futile, and the reflection turned his gaze back upon the scene in a way that felt mocking and claustrophobic. Finding this inversion of purpose disturbing, he surreptitiously moved his eyes away from his own reflection and toward that of his companion. Hazy and indistinct, the stark triangularity of the shoulders of his suit and its formless grey color played with the blank, cream smudge that passed for his face in the window. It suggested a distortion of the human form, the subsuming of the person into the role of the clothing. Faceless, cold.

The sudden strobe of a row of lights at a station outside effaced both figures, and again the train was a part of a larger world.

"I see you survived the bombardment." The other surprised James by speaking first.

"Yes, well, he was a concerned citizen. Very concerned. I—" A rough bit of rail shook James, but his companion's body swayed effortlessly with the motion. *A true traveler, too.*

James finished his thought, mimicking the dry delivery of the other man: "I consider it a privilege to speak with such people."

"And you emerged victorious or defeated?" If he had detected the hint of irony in James's voice, he did not let on.

"Well, I believe I left the gentleman more broad-minded than when I found him."

"You politely dodge the question by giving me instead a

moderate platitude. You are *indeed* a diplomat." A smile emerged on his featureless face, enlivening it considerably. "Paul Schmitt, how do you do?"

A rapport developing, James responded with his own name as he reached for the menu. He felt the skill with which the man was engaging—a true salesman, likely warming up for a pitch of some type. Well, if his companion were to practice his craft in the lounge, James figured, he had better get in a bit more practice of his own. "And do you require similar diplomacy? I wasn't kidding—it's my job to answer precisely those kind of questions."

His response was more interesting than James anticipated. "What do you make of the balance of forces? If the Russians move on Berlin, are our resources plentiful enough to push them back east without the bomb, or will we have to use it?"

Rule one: When you get something unexpected, stall for time by commenting on the question itself. "That's a very sophisticated question, if you don't mind me saying." Having decided on Pullman's own 'Illinois Sandwich' of corned beef and sausage paired with another Gibson, James replaced the menu and marked his choice on the card provided.

"Not at all," the man replied with a cool smile, withdrawing as he spoke a cigarette from a large silver case. He asked for a light, tapping the small white cylinder on the case lid in preparation. Though he rarely smoked, James made it a practice to carry matches and was able to oblige him by pulling a matchbook he had picked up on the *Queen Mary* from his waistcoat. He ignited one of its contents, lit the other's cigarette, and sat the book to the side in case there was further need.

As the attendant arrived to take the orders of both men, the train slowed to a stop for the large station at Newark. For a moment, the storm was gone, hidden above the sheltered train shed. Paul placed his order—an Old Granddad bourbon and a cold salmon platter—without taking up the menu James had returned. Though he might have checked it when he first sat down, James surmised that he hadn't touched it and likely ordered from memory.

As the attendant retreated, James decided to avoid the politics and instead probe his opposite. "Do you travel frequently, Mr. Schmitt?"

"Indeed I do. Here and there. Day and night. Always laboring on behalf of my betters, always ensuring the client is happy." He smiled, "Actually, I think of myself as a diplomat of sorts, in a way." A pause. "But I'm sure that's nothing like real diplomacy."

"Less dissimilar than you might think. I'm probably too junior to qualify as a real diplomat, but I travel frequently in Europe, consulting with allies, monitoring programs, conveying messages."

The attendant returned with their drinks. As he began mixing James's Gibson, Paul commented, "And now you do much the same thing inside your own country."

"Yes, I begin in a few days."

"St. Louis, yes?"

"Yes, you heard right. I've never been there, but I know Chicago fairly well."

"Chicago." Paul paused. "Actually, I travel to St. Louis myself tomorrow. *Clients.*" The last word was spoken with such an emphasis that marked it as clearly self-explanatory, and a wide-open smile lit up his face as if to underscore the point. James did not inquire further, though something about it intrigued him.

"Oh, yes? Do you continue from Philadelphia, then?" James asked instead, knowing that the Pennsylvania Railroad on which they presently travelled ran its first-class trains to the west through Philadelphia or Baltimore.

"No, actually. Like you, I'm in Washington for the day tomorrow and depart from there. I assume you travel on the B&O?"

James nodded. Like most government employees, his travel from Washington westward was generally on the Baltimore & Ohio Railroad. He sipped his martini before replying.

"Yes, the *National Limited*," he said, naming that road's premier train to St. Louis. "I booked the tickets via telegram when I boarded the liner, though I probably needn't have bothered to book early given the time of year."

Paul offered a grunt of agreement and replied, "I'm on the same train. A fine experience, the *National*." Lights shifted outside as the *Constitution* glided smoothly out of the station. Again, rain beat upon the windows.

Thence followed several minutes of conversation comparing the various roads travelling west from the east coast. The men found much to discuss, as Paul apparently used Cincinnati as one of the hubs of his travels and had ridden them all. James grew increasingly curious about what line of work Paul was in, but so fluid was the conversation that he found no natural break in which to insert the subject.

The arrival of the meals—Paul's mound of flaked salmon on lettuce atop a small silver platter and James's sandwich on a luncheon plate decorated with orange and gold patterns laid against green foliage—momentarily cut off conversation. They ate in silence for a few moments, James savoring the taste of the sausage and beef along with the caramelized mayonnaise prepared for it on the side. It was a simple, hearty, meaty dish the likes of which he had missed while in Europe. He varied his chew, taking in every bite at a leisurely pace. He noticed Paul's manner was much more efficient, even economical, as he carefully and quickly plucked salmon and sides from his platter and brought it to his mouth. The way he ate was curious, as though he were a hungry man pressed for time even though his clothing and manner suggested otherwise. *A starving man under the gun*, James thought to himself.

Perhaps feeling James's eyes upon him, Paul excused himself and headed toward the kitchen, likely in search of a lavatory the next car over. James paused in his enjoyment of the sandwich and gazed out the window. The rain had slackened slightly, but lightning still flashed in the distance. He surmised the train was approaching Trenton, the last major city before Philadelphia. A moment later, his guess was proven correct as the train slid to a halt at a station.

Paul returned a few minutes later, after the *Constitution* had already departed Trenton and returned to its maximum speed. The ride was smooth, and James spared a thought for the catenary overhead supplying the train's electricity as natural electricity continued to occasionally light up the sky outside.

"We never finished our discussion of the Russians earlier," Paul said in a businesslike manner as he reached for the change tray the attendant had left him. "Do you think the bomb will be the only weapon capable of stopping Stalin?"

James inhaled. "I hope it doesn't come to that. The situation in Europe is complex, and the atom bomb would be a very messy way of disentangling it. I do think, however, that we must aid our allies there and be willing to use the bomb to do so if necessary. America cannot abandon the western half of Europe to Stalin, or to anyone, if it's to remain safe and prosperous. We don't wish the Russians ill, whatever our criticisms of their policies in the occupied zones, but we have an obligation to our friends and ourselves to make good on the sacrifices of the last war."

James smiled, a practiced, soothing gesture. Paul, having placed his payment on the tray, seemed rapt. Was that a slight shiver at the mention of the sacrifices of the war?

He continued, "It's our job as diplomats to make it clear to the Russians and everyone else just how important that part of the world is to the United States. That way, by making our intentions clear peacefully, with words, we will hopefully be able to avoid having to make them plain with violence."

For once, the smooth voice across from him had no immediate comeback. Paul paused, drawing himself up slightly as though considering James's words with his whole body. His head bobbed slightly, though it did not nod. "An interesting position, James. You truly believe this, or is this merely what you are supposed to say to your…concerned citizens?"

"Truly, I do believe it."

Paul paused. "Your position has the virtue of a defensive framing, which carries with it a degree of moral superiority. I imagine that's useful in diplomacy. Though, I suppose the simplicity of violence sometimes has its place as well."

Silence hung in the air for a moment before Paul released them both from the semi-trancelike state of somber contemplation that had taken hold. "Well, I believe I'll go enjoy the remainder of this little trip from my seat. I've enjoyed speaking with you. Since we both travel on the same train tomorrow, perhaps we might meet again."

He paused, and fixed his eyes on James. "I enjoy the observation car in the evening, preferably after the second seating for dinner, when it's quieter." His tone indicated an invitation.

"As do I. I usually take the second seating myself. Shall we dine together?"

"Alas, no. I will probably have work to take care of during the regular dinner hour, so I'll find something in one of the lounges. But, the observation afterward?"

"Certainly. Until tomorrow," James replied. Rising slightly as

Paul rose to leave, they exchanged firm nods in lieu of handshakes. Outside, the rain began to lift as the *Constitution* glided to a halt at Philadelphia's 30th street station. As Paul strode off back down the car, James examined the bill and made his payment.

Weary of public diplomacy on rails, James returned to his seat and swiveled it directly at the window as the train departed Philadelphia. He gazed out at islands of light riding high on an expansive sea of darkness as the train resumed its southward journey.

CHAPTER THREE

WASHINGTON, D. C.

Rising early the next morning at Willard's Hotel near the White House, James breakfasted greedily and composed a few obligatory arrival telegrams to family and friends. He then dressed, packed, and set out for the State Department's new headquarters at Foggy Bottom on the Potomac. The last time James had visited the nest, it was still located in the old executive office building next to the White House shared by many government agencies. An outdated and crowded facility, it had been determined that the emerging American diplomatic machine required far larger quarters all its own, and it was to that building that James now repaired.

Meetings followed. Meetings all morning, and meetings most of the afternoon. Under-secretaries and deputies and Foreign Service officers of all stripes briefed and debriefed him. Memoranda were taken and given. Hands were shook. The importance of his task was impressed upon him more times than he could count. The secretary himself, though unavailable to actually meet that day, was counting on him, he was told.

By the end of it, James was more than ready for the isolation offered by a long train journey.

A cab ride deposited him and his luggage at Columbus Circle, the plaza in front of the neoclassical gateway to the capital, Union Station. More than a dozen magnificent archways, many supported by gigantic columns crowned by statues of Greek gods, majestically beckoned forward travelers to depart through a shining temple of progress and glory.

Stepping through the waiting taxis, he reached the grand arcade under the arches and columns, the narthex of the Station. James paused here, at the threshold, to admire the view behind him. There was the Capitol dome, intentionally framed by those archways to awe and inspire passengers arriving into the city, supplicants on the pilgrim road to democracy. It felt cleansing, and with a last deep breath, he was ready to depart.

Crossing through the brass doors into the nave that was the Great Hall, James found his gaze pulled upward to the vaulted ceilings gilded in gold. Again, more classical statuary gazed down at the travelers lounging on the carved wood benches or traversing hurriedly the marble floor below. The hum of dozens of conversations and the patter of hundreds of feet echoed off the vaulting and created a sort of monastic chant, a liturgy of the hours said in honor of the gods of transportation day and night amidst a great rail terminal. James, a mere novice amidst the throng of initiated—commuters, politicians, salesmen—set off toward the ticket window, the sounds of his own footfalls contributing their small part to the sacral symphony.

Maneuvering through the mass, he arrived at the window for the Baltimore & Ohio Railroad, the oldest and most-old fashioned of the American roads. There, the ticket agents exacted their priestly tolls for access to the concourse beyond. Removing cash he had stowed in his jacket for ease of access, he paid for the two tickets he had reserved by telegram: one for the cost of carriage on the railroad, the other for a sleeping berth in a Pullman. Once they were firmly in hand, he checked his luggage, keeping only his 'grip', a well-worn, well-constructed leather travelling bag containing the essentials for an overnight journey, on his person. Thus prepared, he strolled slowly, at an even and respectful pace, toward the concourse where the trains waited. His measured pace contrasted with that of the crowd around him, which surged this way and that with a haste that disregarded the majesty of the place.

Massive iron fences and gates separated the concourse and its waiting passengers from the object of adoration: lined up before James were the great named trains of the promising American century, specials and expresses and limiteds, each assembled with their observation cars facing the iron gates that would not be rolled back until the communion of boarding began. Hanging off the back of each were 'drumheads'—pictorial sigils of storied names and glorious routes. There sat the Pennsylvania's *Liberty Limited* on the verge of departure for Chicago and its competitor, the B&O's grand *Capitol Limited.* A dozen other trains bound for far-off destinations, cloaked in haughty names and bearing the hallmarks of speed and refinement, lined the platforms. Here were the chariots of progress champing at the bit to unlock their brakes and whisk the great—and the merely good—to the promised horizon.

Waiting for the ritual of boarding to begin, James examined the Pullman ticket he had purchased. Government employees generally occupied the lowest level of sleeper accommodation—the open 'section' of a convertible day couch that became a bed curtained-off from the corridor at night—for the simple reason that the government was only willing to pay the lowest rate for professional travel. Since sections were shared with one other person—a fold-down 'top bunk' accommodated the passenger who had paid less—travelers selecting this option had to be prepared for anything and any*one*. Fresh from Europe, however, James was willing to foot the extra cost of an upgrade to a private room, a $17.45 surcharge on top of the $35.95 fare for carriage in a Pullman. His ticket, colored a simple white, correctly indicated a compartment berth all to his own.

Finally, it began. The crush of passengers congregating outside the gate proudly advertised for the *National Limited* seemed to collectively exhale as the iron fence was swung back and they started forward. The supplicants, thinking only of themselves and their destination, thronged together with collective haste as they pushed ahead. Pulling on his watch chain, James saw that it was exactly 6:15—the precise time boarding should begin for the scheduled 6:30 departure.

Sliding into the crowd, James steered himself down the platform, taking the train in as he walked. It seemed to stretch out into infinity, boldly exceeding in length even the platform shelters of the station. Thirteen cars comprised it, an assortment of modern lightweight equipment, streamlined and spare with touches of aluminum and stainless steel; classic heavyweight equipment modernized and 'streamstyled' by the railroad to better fit *au courant* art deco aesthetics; and unreconstructed all-steel heavyweights still plying the rails, unrepentant, after decades of service. Colors jumped out: Pullman green on the older, heavier cars; a splash of bone white and cheerful blue on one of the 'foreign road' sleepers bound for destinations beyond the B&O; and, above all, the tasteful, conservative blue and grey of the B&O on most of the equipment.

It was an impressive sight. Moving forward, James paused to admire the observation car at the train's rear. The purpose of the car was to combine luxury sleeping-car space with an intimate cocktail lounge; James knew it contained a few large sleeping berths and a 'solarium' with extra-tall windows at its rear allowing those enjoying its lounge a better view of the scenery. Though owned and operated by Pullman, it was specially outfitted for service on the *National Limited* and was painted beautifully in B&O's colors. Its drumhead was the capitol dome logo of the railroad, a logical bit of advertising given its strategy of capturing the governmental officials and tourist market to Washington. On either side of the dome drumhead was 'the *National Limited*' spelled out with raised gold lettering in a sleek script. The car bore the name *Capitol Escort* on its side.

Beyond it stood no fewer than five sleeping cars. Strolling down the platform, he brushed his fingertips against the *Escort*, feeling its cold steel and the contours of its rivets, before angling away from the train to get a better look. Next in line was his own home for the trip, the heavyweight sleeper *Loch Awe*, an old carriage whose steel frame had been modernized with an aerodynamic roof and rounded windows. Several more sleepers of varying configuration sat forward of his car, and he made out at least one modern, lightweight aluminum carriage in the bunch. Squinting toward the horizon at the end of the platform, he could also see a dining car, what looked like three coaches and, at the very front of the train, the 'head end' complement of a combined baggage-lounge car, a railway post office sorting car, a shabby-looking express parcel shipment car wearing a faded green, and two large diesel engines with streamlined bodies painted in blue, white, and grey.

An even more colorful crowd of hurried about, seeking their carriages. The mixture, as one would expect for this train, was heavy on uniformed military officers from each of the branches and conservatively-suited men—probably businessmen or, like James, government employees heading west—mixed in with a few fashionably dressed ladies attired in well-cut coats and couture hats. The better-attired congregated, like James, at the rear to board sleepers, while an only slightly less formal flock of passengers streamed further down the platform to board the coaches. The air was thick with the fumes of a dozen running diesel engines and the conversation of a thousand gaggling humans; intermixed, they drifted up into the air, perfumed offerings to the gods keeping watch outside.

"It's this car, I think."

"Further down, further down."

"I don't think we have time. You'll just have to make do."

"It's so *long*."

"I promise I'll telegram when I get there."

"Porter, help me with this bag!"

Taking it all in, James smiled at a little girl, no more than four, cautiously walking down the platform holding her mother's hand. She looked up at the train with a mixture of awe and fear. James smiled at her, remembering his own childhood love of the great steel beasts that opened up the world. She saw his smile and returned one of her own, the two strangers united in their appreciation for the experience they were about to share.

Behind this pair briskly walked a trim young woman clad entirely in black save for her stark golden hair. All business, she made her way directly up the platform, casting her eyes over the train only to identify the car names. Clearly, she was no romantic when it came to travel, though she herself seemed remarkably glamorous even in her sombre clothes. Her chin had an aristocratic tilt and her lips were full and red, while her naturally fair skin seemed enlivened by a rich sun tan. James turned slightly to track her as she walked to the vestibule of the *Escort* and boarded without so much as a glance up the platform at the rest of the scene.

His attention momentarily stolen by the striking woman, James failed to notice the body of another passenger carelessly careening for him. Only a snippet of conversation warned him of the impending collision: "Yes, yes, uh, right here dear—"

James whipped his neck around in time to get just a hint of a short, squat body belonging to a middle-aged man dressed dapperly in pinstriped black. Then that person rammed James with his considerable bulk, sending them both to the platform. Pullman porters came running from up and down the platform as the two men disentangled themselves amidst a flurry of apologies.

"I'm so sorry to have bowled you over like that," the stranger said, hurriedly and perhaps a bit too earnestly.

"Not at all, my fault for pausing while everyone is trying to get on board," James replied, though his true feelings agreed that the man had blundered badly.

As the porters helped both men to their feet and began brushing off their jackets, a short, equally squat woman dressed in a dowdy grey dress with a pink floral pattern grasped the arm of the pinstriped man and practically shouted at James, "I'm so sorry, sir! My husband was just trying to figure out where we're going! He can be such a klutz!"

James reddened slightly as the woman continued to shout her apologies, throwing in the odd condemnation of her husband's clumsiness for flavor. He loathed causing a fuss in public, and yet he found that rather a scene was forming nonetheless, complete with multiple bystanders and official assistance. Beyond the porters, even a random man in a shabby brown overcoat had rushed up to and stopped before the little tableau, though his arms hung uselessly at his sides and his expression seemed to indicate that he was at a loss as to what to do.

"Thank you, everyone, but I'm fine," James said. Addressing the porters and the man in pinstriped black, he added, "I'm really fine, everyone. You gentlemen can certainly return to your duties, thank you for your help."

"Wait," interjected the pinstriped man. "Could one of you porters direct us to our room?" His wife produced a ticket for examination and one of the porters responded, "Why, sir, you're right here in the observation car, let me help you on board." Putting action to words, he extended a hand to steady the man and waved the couple toward the carriage. The two squat figures, now with an official escort, made their way up the stairs and into the *Capitol Escort*.

The man in the brown overcoat remained fixated as this little scene played out, a scowl upon his face and a prominent scar on his cheek catching James's attention. Finally, he turned back down the platform toward the station. James felt his eyebrow arch as he watched the figure retreat: *perhaps he had forgotten something*?

As though to brush away the unpleasantness, James tossed a glance over his shoulder and was struck by the imposing figure of a man of medium build wearing a well-tailored suit in a tasteful green tweed. The first thing about him that drew the eye was the scant trapezoid of a mustache that crowned his upper lip. Having been drawn in by the mustache, the eye was immediately drawn upward to the large, Gallic nose surmounting it, its slight downward droop making it appear as though the mustache cowered beneath its shade. A neat little homburg covered a mixture of black and silver hair, suggesting a man in late middle-age. His eyes were a rich brown; a tiredness lurked beneath them, but also a peculiar sharpness—a hardness, even, unforgiving and censorious—as they observed the scene that had just played out before them. The continence he wore suggested disapproval, though that might merely have been the effect of the remarkable resemblance that James only now comprehended.

Good heavens, James thought, *he looks exactly like a 2/3-sized Charles de Gaulle!*

James should know—he had seen the famous French general several times in Paris, and he was transfixed at the resemblance. Only the height and build of the figure before him failed to match that of the famously-imposing Frenchman; his doppelganger, in contrast, couldn't be more than five feet and nine inches and seemed to be built rather trimly. *That nose, though, that mustache*, he thought to himself, *surely he must be playing this up intentionally! Perhaps he's an actor on the stage, an impressionist. Or maybe a relation of de Gaulle—a diplomat on leave, maybe?* Wild speculations poured through James's mind as he contemplated this exotic sight.

Only when those brown eyes traversed from the figure of the departing man in the brown coat to fix on James himself did it occur to James that he was staring. He summoned a weak smile, at which the doppelganger arched an eyebrow before turning away and starting back up the platform.

Shaken by these events, James considered retreating to his cabin. Retrieving his watch once more, he saw that the train was only minutes from departure. He replaced it and took one last look down toward the concourse.

There was the man in brown pushing his way back through the iron gates, nearly colliding with a vision in red trying to pass through in the process. James was immediately struck—a red pillbox hat with a hint of veil worn at a fashionable angle, a red jacket cut to fit her trim, slight figure, and red, four-inch heels. *Italian*, James thought, referencing the heels rather than the woman. Only her stockings—a conservative nude brown—and her bag—an oddly-dissonant black—disrupted the symphony of pure, passionate color playing out in her wardrobe.

Her baggage porter followed close behind, toting a nondescript brown suitcase and struggling to keep up as she finally squeezed through the iron gates and hurried up the platform. The distinctive red cap of the porter's uniform coincidentally matched the color of his client, making the scene even more mesmerizing. She rushed to the entrance to the *Capitol Escort*, waving her hand at the Pullman porter standing just outside as she ran. A whistle sounded from further up the platform and the conductor's call of "All aboard!" soon followed.

Having had enough close encounters for one day, James took a last look at the magnificent enterprise that was the *National Limited* before taking a few short steps to his own carriage, the *Loch Awe*. There, one of the tall Pullman sleeping car porters that had aided him only moments earlier welcomed James aboard and introduced himself as Lucius. Helping him up the steps, he directed James to turn to the left as he entered and make himself at home in room B, a 'compartment' accommodation consisting of a private room, bed, and toilet all packed into a tiny berth.

James always liked compartments. Though smaller than the expansive drawing room accommodations that served the wealthiest travelers, they provided more than enough space and comfort for their cost. Most importantly, they had the virtue of privacy, including a door and bulkheads instead of the curtains that divided the cheaper section beds.

Surveying his cabin, he first glanced out its window, located directly across from the door. He then turned to his left and tossed his grip onto the long couch that ran perpendicular to the tracks, filling an entire wall. Lucius would make it up into his bed later that night. There was also an armchair situated across from the couch, a mirror, and a sink that folded down from the wall. A second bed, a 'top bunk' situated parallel to the tracks, could also fold down from the ceiling if needed.

His inventory of the cabin complete, James felt a slight jolt signaled that train was departing—he quickly consulted his watch—precisely on time at 6:30. Ahead lay a journey of twenty hours through the valleys of western Maryland, the mountains of West Virginia, and the plains of the Midwest.

Searching through his grip for a toothbrush, James discovered yesterday's newspaper. He removed it, tossing it into the waste bin by his sink. Its ominous headline glowered back at him from the trash.

Good riddance, he thought. *Enough of that for a few days.*

CHAPTER FOUR

The *National Limited* was racing through the Washington suburbs as the last traces of the sun disappeared from view. Only the rhythmic rocking of the rails and the occasional specks of light outside the window interrupted the velvety dark of the cloud-covered night. The muffled thud-*thud*-thud of the wheels upon the rail beat out a steady tempo enlivened by the Bacchic improvisation of the engine's horn far in the distance.

Anticipating the arrival of the conductors to check his ticket, James had left his door ajar after settling in. Lucius had then oriented him to train: "observation lounge to your rear, club car lounge at the front, diner in the middle," he had said with a smile.

"It really is a rolling community," James had mused in response. "Different places to eat, to drink, to talk."

"Oh, yes indeed," replied Lucius with a deep, smooth accent of Georgia or the Carolinas, "and folks of all types, too, just like any old village in the land."

"I imagine you've seen your share of village idiots," James prodded with a slight grin.

"Mr. Brummell, I could talk your ear off on that score…

but then I wouldn't be much of a porter!" Both men laughed, knowing that discretion was perhaps the paramount virtue of his profession.

Lucius departed, and James resumed his gazing at the nothingness beyond the window. The engine's horn bellowed ahead, a herald of the passing of the steel giant demanding that all give way before it. It knew of its importance, its mission. It was more than a collection of rivets; it was rather a mass of humanity in motion, an embodiment of the progress of the species up from darkness and its gradual conquest of nature and barbarism. Aboard were people from every walk of life, swept up at the giant's pleasure into one of a dozen carriages and classes and compartments governed by customs and etiquettes all their own, molded by its hand into a community made up of a hundred little societies of meals taken and conversations forced and glances exchanged, and finally discharged from its embrace back out into the world, never to be seen together again. Like an exotic flower that blooms only briefly before perishing, each such journey disclosed a beauty and wonder made tragic by its ephemeral nature.

The arrival of the conductors to check his tickets stirred James from his reverie by reminding him that even rolling metaphors can be afflicted by quotidian bureaucratic rituals. He gave both papers over, the B&O carriage paper to the B&O conductor—the man overseeing the movement of the train as well as the B&O's own signature dining car—and the Pullman ticket to the Pullman conductor—the man responsible for overseeing the operations of the sleeping and lounge cars. Both were taken and validated, leaving James with a stub check from each to serve as proof of his payment. He pocketed them with semi-seriousness, expecting to see them again in a few months when his hand again strayed into that particular pocket in search of a half-forgotten candy, or a pen that was not there, or—in derelict hope—for a coin gone astray.

The ritual concluded, James rose and exited his room, shutting the door behind him. The time had come for him to explore his conveyance in the same manner an anthropologist might seek after some lost tribe of the Andes. He would begin at the apex of the social pyramid; the corridors were clear, and he turned left to start toward the observation car. Being second-to-last in the train's consist meant that he only had to travel a few feet before exiting the *Loch Awe* and entering the *Capitol Escort.*

James made his way down a narrow corridor as he entered. On his left were several large sleeping accommodations similar to his own compartment. The rhythmic pounding of the wheels outside suddenly increased in tempo. Unsteady at the higher speed, James rocked to his left, his large frame gently bumping one of the compartment doors. Unfastened, it opened slightly and revealed a field of red through the open slat. James thought he recognized the outfit of the striking woman from the platform, but his pace carried him quickly past the door and he restrained the urge to crane his head backward to confirm his suspicion. Past these rooms and the kitchen area in the middle of the car was the lounge. Extra-large windows and plush seating invited those within to sit, eat, drink, discuss, and—above all—to enjoy the scenery passing by and the view down the track behind the train.

It being early in the journey and already dark out, there were only a few passengers present. James sat toward the very back in an armchair and ordered a dry California sherry from the Pullman attendant. Moonlight had begun to shine through the cloud cover outside, and James could almost make out the scenery of western Maryland outside. He glanced over his shoulder; there, behind him, he knew lay the Potomac River. A stray moonbeam glanced off the surface of the water, confirming his theory. A light snow cover graced the ground around it.

Sipping his drink, he surreptitiously surveyed his fellow passengers. Seated in the corner at the rear—across the car and to James's right—was the striking blond woman he had seen on the platform. Then, he had had but a glimpse. Now, he was able to observe her more closely. She wore a conservative black dress with a hint of dark black brocade and a matte black hat from which emerged thick waves of blonde hair. Only a silk ribbon of cream on the hat and the golden hue of the hair spoiled the uniformity of color. *Expensive*, James thought, taking in both the outfit and the woman wearing it. She had green eyes and skin that might have been naturally pale but still bore proudly the remnants of a suntan lurking just beneath the surface. Her cheekbones were high, and she radiated a beauty that was almost aristocratic. The oppressiveness of the her head-to-toe black interacted with the refined beauty of her bone structure—and the hint of wildness suggested by the slowly fading tan—to produce an effect that was both intriguing and somewhat unsettling. Her body language was closed off, her legs tightly placed together, shoulders straight, her hands in her lap neatly holding a long black clutch. The attraction he felt to her was not erotic, but rather the sort of contemplative admiration one feels for a brilliant, but somewhat unsettling artwork found unexpectedly in a museum.

Then it hit him: *mourning clothes*. She had lost someone recently. Very recently, judging by the darkness of the black. Making no move to acknowledge James's arrival, she stared instead aimlessly into the night, perhaps noticing, like James, the moonlight on the Potomac. *Perhaps a widow, unreceptive to the casual conversation of a bachelor?* he speculated.

Sipping his drink to cover, he traversed his eyes to the left and observed a tall, handsome man of dark, almost olive complexion reading a newspaper. He wore a naval uniform with the rank of Lieutenant-Commander, and his thick, black hair seemed just long enough to flirt with military impropriety. A young—very young, James thought—face was obscured by the newspaper. From the uniform alone, though, James recognized him as the man in the compartment next to his own. He also recognized the two empty glasses on the small table next to him and a third, full of what appeared to be Scotch, in his hand. *Good Lord,* James thought to himself, *we've only been on the train half an hour!*

The subject sensed he was under observation. Looking up from his drink and paper, he smiled broadly—a recruiting poster smile, if there had ever been one. Raising his glass slightly in acknowledgment, he addressed his watcher.

"Gotta have some fun while in motion, right?"

James mirrored the gesture with his small sherry glass, "Oh yes, Commander…"

"Mario. Mario Tollo, that is." The smile somehow grew even wider. "U.S. Navy," he said, raising the glass to his temple in mock salute, "but I won't stand on ceremony. Glad to meet you Mr…."

"Brummell, but you can call me James. State Department." Both men drank.

"Seems like everybody on this train is a g-man like us, huh?" There was a strange, pre-packaged quality to his speech. He loosed a low, breathy exhalation and took another drink.

The breaks squealed outside the carriage and James felt his body tugged toward the front of the train as it suddenly slowed. Turning to look over his shoulder, the sparkle of the moonlight on the water illuminated a curve in the river that the track was following. A bright flash of light outside was followed quickly by a massive black engine hauling a long freight train. The view was blocked, nature giving way to the practicality of the railroad business.

"Yeah," James finally replied, "but you and I at least upgraded to compartments. Most of our brethren are stuck in the sections."

"Uncle Sam's stingy, that's for sure. For me, though, I always say make every journey an occasion." James did not doubt him. Suiting action to words, he downed the last of his Scotch and signaled to the attendant for another.

Noticing the submarine service insignia on the man's blue uniform, James probed. "You were at sea recently?"

Mario paused only a moment. "Yes." He gulped, perhaps contending with his last snort. "Yep. Love sailing. Love the ocean." The attendant arrived with another sealed mini-bottle of whisky and poured it. "All during the war, too. I've been stationed at Norfolk just recently, though. Good to be back on land—er, rails, or whatever." He tilted his glass toward the train, a gesture of respect. "You a…diplomat, or something?" His voice revealed a trace of an accent of New York, perhaps the Bronx.

James outlined his purpose for the submariner. The standard questions followed, and he gave the standard replies. He was a strange conversant, his personality rather intense and sometimes distracted. Perhaps it was just the whiskey.

Having finished his drink, Mario set off for what he claimed would be dinner, though the unsteadiness with which he rose suggested he might be better off resting in his cabin. As for James, with his sherry glass running dry and no other specimens to observe in his immediate vicinity, he paid his bill and rose to leave. With the train only minutes from crossing over into West Virginia—still a 'dry' state after all these years—he knew asking for a second drink would have been, at any rate, futile. The spirits would shortly be locked away until Ohio.

The limited jolted slightly as it slowed to pass through a small commuter station. James leaned over to try to make out the name but the velocity was too great and the light too scant.

The sound of a discrete cough caused him to snap upright. There, standing in the aisle alongside him, was the woman in red from the platform. No longer in her hat, James was struck by the lustrousness of the jet-black hair she wore in a low chignon gathered at the nape of her neck. Her eyes were a dark brown, almost black, and her skin a refined, unspoiled porcelain.

"Um, excuse me," she said with a practiced half-smile. Her tone was that of any experienced traveler attempting to navigate around inexperienced gawkers.

Embarrassed at his discourtesy, James leaned backward to allow her to pass. "So sorry, I forgot myself," he offered.

"Not at all," she replied. "This train is so empty it's easy to stretch out and forget ourselves." With that, she moved past him and sat across from the woman in black, whose gaze had remained fixed throughout.

Suddenly regretting his displayed intention to leave—after all, the young lady in question had just sat in the seat next to his own—James hesitated slightly before turning to his left and retreating down the car. The opportunity to make conversation was uncertain—some travelers preferred a convivial train, but others sought solitude—and he knew his pride would be wounded were he to reoccupy the seat he had so publicly vacated. That only a few other people would have noticed did not enter into his calculations—James was a stickler when it came to his own pride, and abhorred a public lapse or reversal of any type.

He paused at the threshold, reconsidering. It was, after all, a long journey and he was, after all, rather fond of the prospect of conversation with such a handsome woman. He turned, gathering himself to return, but immediately noticed that the lady in red had already begun a conversation with the woman in black, whose countenance had lost, at least momentarily, its earlier distance. To his credit, his first thought upon surveying this scene was *Good for her—someone should try and cheer up that poor grieving woman.* His second was less laudatory: *missed my window. Damn.*

He turned once more and exited the car.

* * *

A train the size of the *National Limited* has 'neighborhoods' of sorts. The nicest part of town is, of course, the first-class sleeper accommodation available toward the back of the train, especially in the rooms of the observation car or in the first-class section of James's own carriage. Having briefly explored this area, James was determined to slum it a bit, so after resting for a time in his room—and waiting for the first seating for dinner to be well underway—he set out for the small lounge at the front of the train.

Turning right down the narrow corridor outside his room, he made his way 'train forward' by maneuvering between the corridor's windows on the left and the private rooms of other large sleeping berths on his right. The corridor quickly zagged toward the center of the carriage as he entered the second-class sleeping area of open 'sections', or day couches. At night, these couches would fold down to create one bed, while another would drop down from the ceiling. Curtains—not bulkheads—would serve to seal the sleeping compartments off from one another and grant the occupant some privacy.

Walking forward through this portion of his own car, a sudden lurch of the train caused James to stumble slightly at the first row of couches. There, he noticed the green-suited de Gaulle doppelganger from the platform sitting by himself in the first section on the left. He seemed absorbed in a collection of what appeared to be business documents; though his head had not moved in reaction to his presence, James could sense he had taken notice of him in his peripheral vision. James offered a friendly smile in case he was indeed looking, but received no acknowledgment and hastily resumed his journey.

His trek took him through four additional sleeping cars before he entered the dining car. Here was the midpoint of the train, and also the convenient separation point between coach and Pullman passengers. Sets of tables seating four guests ranged along each row of windows, and an army of waiters, stewards, chefs, and other train personnel plied the aisle in between. The first seating for dinner was already underway, and James's pace slowed as he worked his way through the car.

Particles of conversation drifted in and out of his ear as he made his way along the aisle:

"No—no no. Mill has it all wrong. He fails to grasp what Burke saw plainly—"

"Crab or fish. I *cannot* decide."

"It's a wasteland. A wasteland."

"Though it really wasn't her fault, you see, her husband—"

"—and four grandchildren: Denise, Mary—"

Moving beyond the diner, three unremarkable coaches with day seating brought his count of carriages to ten. The passengers there were absorbed in books, or sleep, or the nothingness visible right outside the window.

He at last reached the final passenger carriage: the baggage-lounge. Divided into two, the portion nearest the passengers was a Pullman-operated lounge not dissimilar to the one he had ridden from New York; the other half contained space for passenger baggage and a dormitory for the crew. This close to the engine, the bellowing of the horn at grade crossings was particularly prominent, adding urgency and speed and raucousness to the atmosphere. Cigarette smoke gathered at the ceiling; a deck of cards was cut with a crack; a woman laughed immoderately in the corner. This was, if not the heart of the train, then certainly some other vital organ.

James noticed upon entering the familiar figure of Paul Schmitt, still dressed in his grey suit. He sat at a small dining table across from the man in pinstriped black that had bowled James over on the platform. The latter's wife was nowhere to be seen, and empty plates before the two men indicated they had just finished a light supper. James found this point odd; most couples of their age would naturally take dinner in the grand and hospitable surroundings of the diner. *Perhaps they had had a disagreement?*

Looking up, Paul checked his large wristwatch and acknowledged James with a nod before returning his attention to his companion. James returned the nod.

Seating himself on a small couch in the lounge area, he ordered an orangeade—like all cocktails available while the train transited the West Virginia panhandle, nonalcoholic—and settled in to observe the crowd. The lounge was busy with a mixture of coach and sleeper passengers returning from the first seating for dinner and a few, like James, waiting for the second seating.

Paul had risen from his table, leaving his companion behind to handle what appeared to be a dispute with the attendant over the bill. Passing James, he paused and sat on the edge of an adjacent seat.

"Mr. Brummell, I trust your journey proceeds well? How is your section?"

"Oh yes, a splendid train, as we discussed. I upgraded to a compartment, actually, on the *Loch Awe*, toward the back. You?"

"I have a compartment in the observation." He leaned in and

down, slightly. "Right next to the drawing room of my fastidious companion over there," he shrugged his shoulder back toward the table he had left. "He and his wife seem *quite* a pair." He paused, as though considering, and then said rather darkly, "Not the first time I've wished for thicker walls on these trains."

Uncertain what to make of that last point, James instead replied to his comments on the couple next door. "Yes, he bowled me over on the platform earlier. The wife made a bigger scene than the both of us. She might be the biggest character of them all." A sympathetic shiver shook Paul.

"Well, I'm also adjacent to our lovely young woman in red—that makes up for it slightly." A smile and wink lit up his face.

"I saw her on the platform, too," James noted, struggling to keep a lupine grin from marring his pious visage. "Charming style." He paused, switching subjects, "I take it you have just enjoyed dinner?"

"Indeed, a light repast only. *Business*." A slight shrug. "I have a few things to attend to, but shall we meet in the observation car at about 9:00?"

"Certainly, see you there."

"Splendid." With that, he was off.

Hot on Paul's tails was the man in pinstripes. James looked up from his drink as the heavy, rapid footsteps of his approach alerted the whole car to his departure. He immediately noticed that beads of perspiration had formed on the short man's forehead.

As though sensing a need to explain, the man halted in front of James and said in an unsteady, but clearly bitter voice, "These Pullman attendants will rob you blind if you're not careful!"

He paused, expecting a quick reply from James. When none immediately came, he suddenly looked abashed. The redness in his cheeks increased as he mumbled a 'good evening' and resumed his quick pace toward the rear of the train.

It was then James noticed the man in green tweed from his own sleeper standing at the entrance of the car. He had been watching the scene, probably waiting for a seat to open up. The fat man pushed by him, forcing him to contort his body to give the larger man space to push by at his rushed, inelegant pace.

With both Schmitt and his dinner companion gone, the empty space on the couch beside James was finally accessible, and the man in green made his way to it. Again, he noted the resemblance to de Gaulle. Knowing he had been seen this time, James offered him a greeting, "Good evening, *monsieur*." The man wrinkled his nose slightly at the term, perhaps subconsciously, and his mustache seemed to cower at the thrashing of its protector-god.

Whoops, James thought, *I shouldn't have let the French slip through!*

"Yes, good evening," he replied while surveying the lounge. Finding no seats better located, he resigned himself to asking "May I sit?"

"Certainly," replied James, and he scooted to make room on the small couch. "I believe I saw you on the way here—you have a section near the back of the *Loch Awe*?"

"Yes, I'm only traveling to Grafton, so a section to myself is sufficient." A pause. "Of course, I travel on railroad business, so I accept what my pass gets me." His voice was low and a touch weary, a distant cousin of the horn echoing ahead of them.

Do I ask? James thought. *The resemblance is so powerful!*

"What sort of work do you do for the railroad?" he said instead, hastily adding his name by way of introduction.

The older man nodded a greeting in acknowledgment. "Ellicott Robinson." Another pause as he caught the eye of the attendant. "I am with the railroad police." The statement—free of contractions or informality—hung momentarily in the air between them, thickening it to the consistency of sap.

"How interesting," James said evenly. "And do you police the dry laws while we transit West Virginia?" he said, pairing a light smile with a gesture to the rest of the lounge.

Robinson picked at a speck of imaginary lent on his arm, the green tweed aesthetically immaculate and possessing new authority by virtue of its wearer's occupation. "Perhaps." He seemed far away—perhaps up by the horn, which shyly refused to comment; instead, only the sound of the wheels beating against the rails and the omnipresent hum of conversation filled the pause. "My position has to do with everything involving crime on the railroad's property." It was a brittle statement, dry and noncommittal. Beneath it lurked countless possibilities.

The tone Robinson had taken did not invite further scrutiny, so James merely nodded in response. The attendant arrived, addressing him with a mixture of formality and informality as "Mr. Ellicott" and taking his order with alacrity. The tone of their conversation seemed to suggest a long familiarity—a *very* long familiarity. James noticed several other customers had been passed over in Robinson's favor, and from that he deduced this was a person of respect within the company.

Robinson ran a hand over his brow, straightening the thick, yet closely-cropped hair that mustered itself along a receding hairline. It was salt-and-pepper to the core, even more so than the distinctive mustache. His tie was a brown and red madder, beautifully printed onto silk, and his pocket square complemented both the tie and the tweed.

The carriage rocked as the limited clattered over the points of a switch, and James quickly moved his arm to compensate for the shift and keep his drink from spilling. Robinson seemed fixed in place, untouched by the motion. James wondered if the conversation had ended.

Robinson removed a pipe from his pocket and groped for a match. James quickly retrieved a matchbook from his vest and offered a light. Accepting it, Robinson sat back and puffed happily for a moment. He then re-engaged, focusing anew on the younger man. "What work do you do, Mr. Brummell?"

"I'm a government man myself," James offered, "but, of course, most of the passengers on this train seem to be so. State Department, though I'll be spending some time in the States for the time being."

Robinson offered a thin, tight smile—the first such expression James had seen out of him. "Yes, the *National* is an exceedingly popular option for government business in the West." He pivoted slightly to look out the window. "What a pity we traverse the most scenic part of its route in darkness."

"Yes, we're still along the Potomac, aren't we?"

"For the moment. We'll soon turn west to climb the mountains through the center of the state. A glorious wilderness." He sounded wistful.

"You know West Virginia well?"

He paused, considering his answer. "I'm from Baltimore. But I had relations here, and that served to bring me west more than a few times. And railroad business, of course."

"Did you begin your career with the police here?"

"In a manner of speaking." He turned his face squarely toward James. "I solved my first case for the Baltimore & Ohio here."

"Oh really? Were you just out of school?"

"I was twelve years old." He turned his head back to the window. "At the time."

James struggled to remain expressionless as he gauged the man's seriousness. He refused to be baited. "That…must have been quite an experience."

"Indeed. I have had many such…experiences on the railroad."

A voice rang through the carriage: "Second seating for dinner in the diner. Second seating."

Setting down his drink, James groped for his pocket watch in his waistcoat, finding the motion awkward in the relaxed furniture of the lounge; he resolved to attach the watch to the less formal, leather strap he had in his grip and shift it to his front breast pocket before dinner. Finally obtaining and consulting it, he replaced it and said with real feeling, "I regret that's my call. I need to duck into my compartment first, but I'll head in right after—do you dine this evening?" He hoped he could hear more of this man, even if he were nothing more than a stock character: the teller of tall tales on railway journeys.

"No, I prevailed upon the chefs to feed me early so that I could work." The attendant arrived with his drink, which he took. "A task to which I shall return after this respite. Enjoy your dinner—I recommend the cornbread pie."

James rose and nodded, "I appreciate your suggestion. It was…a pleasure speaking with you."

Robinson nodded in return, "*Bon appétit.*" He again shifted to look out the window, his mustache twitching slightly.

James struggled to keep from laughing as he headed for the diner.

CHAPTER FIVE

The dining car of a grand train is a point of intersection. People, sounds, smells, motives; seated, often with a stranger, the passenger is tossed head-first into a sort of sensory mosaic. Noise intrudes when first entering the car, noise from every angle and in every dialect:

"You must understand the *beauty* of Turner as distinct from the *meaning of* Turner."

"Dorothy, pass me the butter."

"They have no pitching. They barely have batting."

"I was once *on* a buoy. Yeah, it was—"

"No, the butter."

"Coffee? I want coffee."

"Yessuh.

"Say, when will they serve whiskey again?"

thud-thud-thud-*thud-thud*-thud-*thud-thud*-thud-*thud-thud*-thud

Then the cacophony subsides, or rather unifies until it is one with the air and the rocking of the carriage and the existence of this curious space racing down the track. James felt it all—each noise, each voice, each movement—as he stepped over the threshold into the car; by the time he had finished blinking, it had all melted together. It was the diner.

A single table sat empty—empty, that is, save for the woman in red. She gazed casually toward the window, a bored, weary look on her face conveying an utter lack of interest in the black cloak of night obscuring the passing scenery. James suspected she really looked at the ghost of her own reflection on the glass. *Perhaps she is vain.* He thought. *Perhaps she merits vanity.* He knew that he would be seated with her before the steward had even asked for the formality of his permission, and he girded himself for the task, perhaps pleasurable, of making conversation.

As he approached, the small, gloved hand that rested lightly on her cocktail glass gripped it and brought it to her lips, painted a cheerful red that played amiably with her porcelain skin. James nodded as he slid into the seat across from her. He appraised their reflection in the window: the man in blue and the woman in red, their postures stiff and proper at this first encounter; the ghosted images of the white table cloth and blue china; the prism of the carafe of water, the glint of the ceiling light off the aluminum trim of the chairs. A flash of light here, a dash of color there, all uncertain and translucent, just as the air was abuzz with half-heard conversations from other tables, a steady din complementing rather than competing with the thudding of the wheels on rails. The aromas of a dozen different dishes levitated above their tables, merging and melding until the scent of the car approximated their average. Even the echo of the horn seemed fuzzy and indistinct this far back, completing the surreality of senses that permeated that moment in the window glass.

She sipped her drink and averted her eyes as she laid it down again, allowing him to notice her long, thick lashes. "Hello again," she said, softly but confidently. "The train doesn't seem so empty when everyone is trying to eat dinner." Her eyes flicked up to look directly at James. So brown, they might as well have been black.

The waiter was pouring spring water from a large bottle sat upon the table as James responded, "No, it doesn't." He paused, adding an element of mock seriousness. "I hope you'll police me if I get in your way again, I *can* be so easily distracted by the scenery." He did not look at the nothingness outside.

The double-entendre provoked a smile from the woman. "And, beyond admiring the *natural* beauty visible only from the train, of course, what brings you here today?" It was his turn to smile.

The ice broken, conversation flowed. He gave his particulars, and she introduced herself as Miranda Credo. She interrogated him on his journey and, discovering he had only just returned from Europe, evinced an appropriately deferential interest in where he had been and what he had done. James, in a more candid moment, would have admitted that he loved playing this particular role—wise master to wide-eyed student, brutish man-of-the-world to innocent *ingénue*. She played her part perfectly, and he found himself enjoying the interaction immensely.

"I bet you've had all sorts of intrigues. Rubbed shoulders with the mighty. Charmed countesses." Her statement made no effort to hide its invitation to regale.

"Oh, a few maybe. The mighty, that is, not the countesses. But I'm mostly a messenger, and a listener." He summoned up his best anecdotes for her—the luncheon at which he heard Churchill describe his time in Cuba under the Spanish, the Council of Foreign Ministers meeting where Secretary Marshall had accused the Soviets of starving the conquered Germans, the mislaid crate of wine that had nearly derailed a meeting with the Italians—trying throughout to avoid or disguise the reality of his very junior status without deceiving her outright. She seemed so eager to know him and what he did that he was at pains to avoid disappointing her.

Though reluctant to abandon such a stimulating course of questioning, he made sure to volley back. Returning west to St. Louis after visiting friends in the Virginia Tidewater, she said. "I toil," she continued with mock seriousness, "in the cesspit of gossip and petty dramas." His eyebrows rose. "I write," she paused, "for newspapers and magazines on fashion, society, and other things of no consequence. Whether that makes *me* inconsequential as a result, I've not yet decided."

"Fascinating!" James said, actually meaning it. "I'm something of a sartorialist myself."

"Yes, *quite* the ensemble you have on this evening," she said, gesturing with her fork. "Saville Row? A grand tailoring house catering to the aristocracy?"

The gentle teasing in her tone did nothing to put him off. "Just off the Row, actually. Jermyn Street. Though lately I've been using a little shop in Paris…"

The salad course gave way to the main as they compared the merits of shoulder-lines and waistcoats. New cocktails, still virgin, replaced the old. Barriers gradually melted and the conversants found themselves smiling, laughing, and exchanging stories easily. The reflected couple in the window glass seemed comfortable with one another, light and airy and entirely absorbed. Their indistinct faces and blotches of blue and red clothing could have been taken from a poster advertising the glamour of travel. James thought her smile beautiful, curvaceous and knowing, hinting at wisdom beyond her years and station. He found himself feeling slightly intoxicated despite the absence of alcohol in his cocktail glass. He did not notice the passing of Robinson, returning from the lounge car, though Robinson certainly noticed the handsome couple so utterly absorbed in one another's conversation.

Picking at the remnants of his dish, James glanced down at the blue and white china on which it was served. Around the rim were illustrations of locomotives, while the centerpiece design depicted the double-tracked route of the train through the Appalachian wilderness. He suddenly felt sad, thinking of the endless loop of the engines around the plate and the loneliness of the forest. The dinner was drawing to a close.

She declined dessert, instead producing a cigarette. James groped for a book of matches, pulling one from his waistcoat. He struck the match, set the book aside, reached across, and lit the small cylinder for her, a time-honored ritual of decent courtesy that hinted more than a little at indecency. Her gloved hand brought it to her mouth, and she inhaled deeply, savoring its flavor. The train had accelerated, perhaps to tackle a grade, and the dining car trembled slightly in keeping with the tempo of the wheels. Silverware left on his plate clattered slightly. It all felt momentous, and a little dangerous.

Haloed in smoke from her exhale, she asked in an even, but low, tone, "Are we safe? Will there be war with the Russians?" She paused, casting her eyes down in a meaningless glance at the blue and white plate before her and continued more slowly, "The papers make things seem very bad, but they also seem… reserved, somehow. I don't know." Her eyes darted back up to look straight at James, "Are we being told the truth?" Those eyes pried into him.

He watched her lips close again around her cigarette before responding. "Will there be war?" He licked his lips, searching for the words. "I don't know. We're trying to keep that from happening. As I travelled around Europe, I spent a lot of time listening and watching, and I can say for certain that there is a lot of hope for peace on all sides. Especially ours." He smiled weakly. "The papers over here get it mostly right, but there's a…gap…

in comprehension. They don't know the Russians, don't know our allies, and don't quite know what to make of our policies. Secretary Marshall has helped, if for no other reason than he is used to dealing with the press and inspires a lot of confidence."

He sipped his water, preparing a summation. She exhaled smoke slowly, distracting him. "We're all trying our best. But, in the end, we're all new at this. The bomb…it changes things, maybe." He silently cursed his equivocation. "There's no one, on either side, who's used to doing diplomacy under these conditions." He leaned back and opened his hands, another unintended gesture of equivocation. "We're all amateurs doing what we can to feel our way through. Some combination of hope and professionalism—clearly communicated between the West and the East—may be enough to keep the peace." He dropped his hands to the table. "Or it might not."

This was not the confidence-inspiring stump speech he was prepared to give to audiences across the U.S. This Miranda drew him in somehow. And then drew something out of him. She was, he decided as she inhaled once more, an entrancing woman.

"It's…honorable of you to speak so plainly to me. I can tell you meant what you just said—that you weren't treating me like the Lady Voters Association of St. Louis or the Rotarians of Boise." She smiled. "Though I'm not sure it makes me feel any better."

"Diplomacy, Miranda, often leaves one feeling that way." He spoke with greater confidence than his experience in that field justified, and deep down he knew it.

They settled their mutual bills with the waiter as the train began to slow. They made the usual niceties one offers on the cusp of a relationship never again to be renewed. But there was a hesitation on both their parts. A hesitation that made James think.

As she rose from her chair to leave, he half-rose from his own and blurted out, "Perhaps you'll enjoy the observation car later?"

"Perhaps I will," she said neutrally. Her eyes met his for a moment, and she was gone.

James slumped back in his seat as she left. Around him, the diner had almost emptied. The train had stopped at a small station, and the lights from the platform illuminated a snowy scene now visible through the window. The reflected couple was gone, banished to memory.

CHAPTER SIX

Ellicott Robinson, special inspector of the Baltimore & Ohio Railroad Police, looked away from the scene in the lounge as he hefted his large pocket watch from his waistcoat. It was a substantial old piece, a railroader's watch. Most men these days had taken to wristwatches, and he found this regrettable. There was something about the weight and the authority of the pocket watch that conveyed seriousness and meaning—particularly on the railroad, where such devices could literally mean the difference between life and death. Similar to most of the carriages on the *National Limited*, weight and wisdom were thought virtuous on the B&O and the company did not rush, like its competitors, to abandon them too quickly in favor of the light, the insubstantial, the modern.

Seeing it was almost 8:30, he replaced the watch and rose from his seat. The young man who had left him a half hour before...Brummell, he said his name was...had carried a pocket watch, and made no effort to forgo ostentation in his manner of consulting it. It had matched his immaculately-cut, but somewhat old-fashioned by contemporary standards, three-piece suit. Robinson smiled to himself; he, too, favored finely-made clothing and he, too, had been subjected more than once to charges of dandyism in his time. He subconsciously ran a finger over his trapezoidal mustache as he turned and exited the lounge.

The train slowed slightly as he moved through the day coaches. It had departed the Potomac and was climbing now, hard, into the mountains of the West Virginia wilderness. Pausing at an empty row of seats, he craned his head down to look out the window. The snow had picked up.

Entering the dining car, he passed through taking surreptitious notice of Brummell absorbed in conversation with a striking young woman in red. The two appeared lost in one another, their mirrored reflections the only other occupants of their little world. Behind them, a naval officer slurred his speech in discussion with a grey-tweeded, bespectacled figure that must surely have been a professor. And then he arrived at the corridor astride the kitchen and Robinson's entertainment came to an end.

Arriving finally at his section, he passed Lucius the porter in the corridor just outside. "Snow is picking up, eh?" Robinson offered.

"Yes, sir, indeed," Lucius replied, "it'll be a rough time over the hills tonight."

"Surely. They'll need the helper more than ever."

"I reckon so, Mr. Ellicott. We'll pick it up at Keyser, as usual?"

"Yes, and not a moment too soon."

"Can I make up your berth for you?"

"Thank you no. I'm only heading to Grafton and, as long as we're not delayed, I'd rather just bed down there. I'll work the rest of the way."

Returning to the reports he had left in his section, he lost himself in them for a time. Figures in the corridor moved through his peripheral vision: blues and greys and blacks, all hazy, indistinct, and of little interest. A stark flash of red in the corridor stirred him some time later. Brummell's companion must have finished before him. Perhaps the conversation had soured?

Consulting his watch, he saw it was late, nearly nine. The prospect of another three hours in motion sobered him. His early dinner right after boarding had been light, and he was already feeling hungry. *Yes,* he thought, *a quick bite in the observation dinette and then back to work.*

Gathering up his papers, he sorted them into the appropriate piles and placed them neatly into the attaché case he had stowed under his seat. A burst of motion in the corridor signaled that the diner had disgorged its remaining patrons; Brummell moved quietly past, nodding at Robinson as he went.

The parade concluded, Robinson retrieved his copy of Caesar's *Gallic Wars* in the original Latin from the grip he had sat on the couch across from him. He had little intention of reading it this evening, but hoped its presence would talismanically ward off potential conversants in the observation lounge. Finally, he pulled a telegram pad from his jacket and began to dash off a note to his department back in Baltimore. Ringing for Lucius, he instructed him to pass it to the train's secretary in the combine car for transmission at the next telegraph point.

The dining tables in the observation car were empty when Robinson arrived, though the lounge was lively. Seated by the attendant, he took note of Brummell conversing with a dull-looking man in a grey suit further down the car, the same one Robinson had witnessed him talking to in the club car earlier. They spoke easily, their postures relaxed and their conversation apparently amicable. Brummell had just received a drink, while the other's glass was nearly empty. Across the aisle, a trim woman decked in mourning black, her beautiful face and golden hair contrasting sharply with her somber clothing, chatted calmly with the professorial-looking figure he had noticed in the dining car. The naval officer sat alone—slouched, really—at the very rear of the train, sneaking sips from a hip flask when he thought no one was looking. Robinson wrinkled his nose in distaste, but made no move to police him.

Ordering an Illinois Sandwich, Robinson slowly poured cream from a little pitcher marked PULLMAN into a large coffee cup decorated in orange foliage. Stirring it with a silver spoon, he kept his eyes cast downward at his cup but opened his ears to the car around him. The thudding of the wheels came at regular intervals, but was less urgent now that the limited had slowed to tackle the steep grades ahead. The Brummell boy was saying something about trains in France while his companion made approving noises; the attendant's voice rang out, offering to replenish his drink, but the other man declined. Raising his eyes slightly, Robinson saw the black-clad woman nodding passively at the low, but sharp remarks of the professor—something about Milton, or was it the Book of Job? Suffering was certainly involved, which probably made for an uncomfortable moment for the mourning woman.

His table shook slightly, and though the train's motion was likely at fault he still found himself turning to look over his shoulder. There, he saw a rather large, sweaty man conversing with the bar attendant. Robinson immediately recalled seeing him in a kerfuffle on the platform at boarding, to say nothing of his close encounter with him in the club car as well.

"No, no," the fat man was saying. "I need a paper from the Midwest. Cincinnati or Chicago." The attendant replied that only the eastern papers were presently available, but that more would be loaded in Ohio. The fat man sniffed, sighed, and huffed back down the corridor. The contents of Robinson's cup agitated again as he walked away. Robinson knew it had to be rough track, but smiled anyway at the coincidence.

A burst of compressed air signaled that the train had entered a tunnel carved into the hillside. The carriage seemed to rock back and forth as the locomotives accelerated into the straight, clear track ahead. The attendant, approaching with a hot pot of coffee to refill Robinson's cup, paused at his tableside until the wheels had properly married to the track at their new speed. The two men shared a knowing glance, a wordless mutual understanding about the virtue of caution on the railroad and the importance of having your 'sea legs' before pouring hot liquid. The carriage finally calmed itself and Robinson nodded his thanks as the attendant returned to the bar, his task complete.

Something moved in his peripheral vision as he nodded, and Robinson turned his head fully around to the right to look over his shoulder. A flash of red. Brummell's young woman—the one he had seen him so engaged with as he had passed through the diner earlier— had stepped into the lounge, but had reversed almost immediately. *Forgotten something?* Robinson thought, *Or just avoiding Brummell?*

Robinson sipped his coffee and regarded the window. Looking past his distorted reflection into the yard of a passing home, he could tell by the flicker of lights from its windows that snow had accumulated deeply here. He consulted his pocket watch and discovered the limited would shortly be approaching Keyser, where the engines would prepare for the steepest and most treacherous leg of the journey.

Again, a flash of red in his periphery as the woman reemerged from the corridor and strode into the car. Seeing her enter, the man opposite Brummell said something to him and rose, offering the lady his seat. She accepted, and the man made his good-nights to both figures, pausing to turn across the aisle and say something to the woman in black as he went. She responded warmly, perhaps glad to have a moment's interruption from the harangues of the professor. The man in grey then made his way forward. As he walked by Robinson on his way out of the lounge, the railroad man was struck by his featureless, expressionless face. He might as well have been performing the most routine and banal of tasks.

The arrival of his sandwich stirred him from his observations. Spreading the caramelized mayonnaise thickly, he began to down it hungrily. Though he often intended to work all the way through his trips for work, he also knew that his boyhood love of dining on rails had never really left him; it consequently drew him to the diners and lounges more frequently than he intended. His green tweed vest had, perhaps, a snugger fit as a result—certainly more so than when he was younger—but he chalked it up as a distinguishing feature of seniority, just like the grey that had crept into his black hair and mustache over the years. *Besides*, he thought to himself as he looked again at the personages assembled in the lounge, *if I've got the show, I might as well have dinner, too.*

And indeed this evening he did, as he continued his remote observation of Brummell and the woman, their reflections of soft blue and stark red silhouetted perfectly within the window while the tunnel blotted out any other stray light. They could have been actors on the stage; her posture, cold and reserved and closed, counterbalanced his, open, leaned-in, and engaged. A distance not present in the diner seemed to have sprung up between them. Then the train emerged from the tunnel and the tableau lost a measure of its magic. Only two young people of uncertain relationship remained.

Some time later, the limited clattered over the points of a switch as he paid the bill, signaling the train's imminent arrival into Keyser. Wiping his mustache with the napkin, Robinson rose and cast a final glance back at the lounge. The professorial figure had gone only moments ago, and the woman in black sat alone and impassive. Brummell's conversation with the woman in red seemed listless at best, and a casual observer might have mistaken them for strangers. The naval officer had left some time before, and, save for a pair of passengers he did not know from one of the forward sleepers, the lounge was otherwise empty. Undoubtedly, the absence of alcohol was to blame for the thin crowd. He turned and started down the corridor. As he made his way back toward his own section, the heavy carriage lurched through a final switch, causing him to brace against the wall; the hot stink of the brakes assaulted his nose just as their screech assailed his ears. The limited had made Keyser at last.

As he crossed from the *Escort* to his own sleeper, he found Lucius at the vestibule door preparing to open it for the station stop.

"I'll step down and stretch my legs," Robinson told him. His book, still unopened, he wedged into his jacket pocket.

"Yes, sir. Last stop until Grafton—I bet no one will need the Oakland stop on a night like this!"

The train came to a stop with a lurch, and Lucius opened the vestibule door. A blast of icy air rushed into the cabin. The platform had been cleared of snow for the limited, but several inches had accumulated on the ground beyond. Following Lucius down the stairs, Robinson stepped off onto the platform and shivered mightily. Only a few passengers emerged from the small brick station to board further up the train. But for a pair of indistinct figures milling about by a distant sleeper, the platform was empty.

The snow was already accumulating on his shoulders, but Robinson's tweed was thick and he resolved to remain outside for a few moments more before retreating back into the steam heat of the carriage. He stamped his feet slightly to warm his legs.

"A bad night for a walk, eh monsieur?" A voice spoke from behind him. *Again, the French? Does he think it's funny?* Robinson thought to himself.

Turning, Robinson addressed Brummell directly. "A night to be grateful you are on a train." He noted no figure in red had followed the young man down.

Both men paused to watch a massive black steam engine work its way up the track adjacent to the limited. It hauled no cars, and its visage amidst the driving snow struck a lonely note.

"I don't suppose we'll be snowed in." Brummell said evenly, adding after a beat "In the mountains." He pulled on a leather strap attached to his lapel, and his pocket watch jumped from his breast pocket. Robinson had noted earlier the other man's struggle to reach the watch in his waistcoat in the lounge, and surmised he had attached it to the leather strap and repositioned it to the more accessible breast pocket sometime in the interim.

"No. Delayed? Perhaps a little. The grades may be slippery." Robinson looked down, shaking the toe of a shoe that had been covered in snow. "This is not deepest, darkest Europe, after all. Or Colorado." Robinson knew tales of trains snowed up for days, especially on the western roads. Indeed, he had been involved in a few himself. But the B&O wouldn't continence such things. "It wouldn't be proper." Robinson mumbled to himself. James cast him a quizzical look, to which he responded, "Never fear, my young friend. The B&O will sweep aside any obstacles in our path."

The two men milled about a moment longer, physically together but alone in their thoughts. Robinson noted a figure in a grey overcoat descending from the *Escort.* Removing a cigarette from a large silver case, he nodded at the detective before turning away to stroll in the other direction, toward the very rear of the train. Robinson placed him as he turned: Brummell's companion in the lounge, the one with the bland complexion.

The lights from the windows up and down the train took on an ethereal, gauzy air as the snowfall intensified. Shadows and figures and blotches of color moved through them, black and blue and a brilliant red: the business of the limited hurrying along inside even as the train itself seemed frozen and still from the platform outside. Faces peered out from the windows of the *Loch Awe* and the other sleepers, drawn momentarily like moths to the pale lights of the station, concern evident on a few at the snow that had clearly accumulated.

Looking over his shoulder, Robinson noticed that the man in grey had reached the end of the *Escort* and stood, silently and still, watching the platform. His expression was concealed by the dark, but the burning tip of his cigarette seemed to reveal the same disinterest with the scene that Robinson had seen on his face in the lounge.

Sounds of a dispute turned the detective's head, and he saw Lucius speaking from his position on the platform to a stout, middle-aged woman still within the vestibule.

"—is very tired," she was saying, her cheeks red more from emotion than the cold air sweeping into the vestibule. "He really must have quiet," she concluded as Robinson inched closer to better hear.

"M'am," Lucius spoke in a tone calculated to appease and reassure, "I understand about the noise, I really do. People comin' to and from the lounge back there, well, they get rocked around by the train in these hills, and they do end up hittin' the door of your drawing room pretty often when they have to turn that corner to get to the next car."

Robinson smiled to himself. It was a common complaint;

the observation car was usually the most sociable car on the train after hours, and its single drawing room was ideally placed for pilgrims to and from the bar to stumble into its bulkheads as they made their way by. The woman, undaunted by Lucius's explanation, continued to enumerate her complaints about the foot traffic, the thinness of the wall separating them from their neighboring compartment, and even the food. Poor Lucius took it all like a veteran under bombardment.

"Sounds like she's gunning for a refund," Brummell said, suddenly appearing beside him.

"Then she's in for a disappointment," Robinson replied. "Porters can no more issue refunds than…well, railroad detectives." As he spoke, the Pullman conductor appeared from further up the platform, likely drawn to the scene by a sixth sense developed over many years on the railroad.

"I don't know…I had a literal run-in with her earlier and she seems like the, er, stalwart type. You know, the ones that squeeze the stone until blood appears?" Though Brummell's words were clearly jovial, his tone seemed subdued.

"A good way to strengthen your fist, perhaps, but useless when the stone in question is trained by the Pullman Company," Robinson dryly remarked. Lifting his gaze slightly, he saw a young face—maybe that of Brummell's lady companion, in fact—peering out one of the Escort's windows. It was gone in only a moment, perhaps slightly ashamed at its curiosity and embarrassed at how little information even an earnest gaze could draw from a near-empty platform nestled in the bosom of a mountain town enveloped in darkness and blanketed by snow.

Turning away from the tableau, the two men strode forward a few steps in silence. The platform was beginning to clear, with the few new riders secure in the coaches and the smattering of sleeper passengers finding the chill too severe for their liking.

The Pullman men seemed to have dispersed the one-woman demonstration that had been blocking the vestibule, and Brummell conceded defeat with a snort, "The stone wins, for once."

With that, Robinson mounted the car and climbed into the vestibule, turning toward his section on the *Loch Awe.* Wordlessly, Brummell followed, breaking off to enter his compartment with a perfunctory "good night" while Robinson continued on down the corridor.

A steam engine's whistle echoed off the mountains, plunging back into the valley whence it had come. A moment later, the *National Limited* jolted. The train dashed forward, daring the snow to stop it.

CHAPTER SEVEN

A sudden, jarring lurch accompanied the screeching, squealing, grinding howl of the breaks as the train brought itself to a sudden halt. Looking up from his work in his section, Robinson first looked out the window but could see nothing save the misty reflection of his own berth. Grabbing for his watch, he saw that it read 12:10 in the morning, twenty minutes outside his destination of Grafton if the train was on time. Surmising from the absence of light outside that the train was still firmly in the wilderness, he settled back in and accommodated himself to the prospect of a delay.

Considering the possibility of reversing course and instructing Lucius to make up his berth into a bed, Robinson demurred. "No, it won't be long." He said to himself. Wedging himself into the corner by the window, he closed his eyes for a moment and heaved a breath as he waited for the train to resume its journey.

***

Rustling in the section ahead of him. A bang on the shared headboard. Robinson's eyes are bleary as he examines yet another report. He rises, and visits the lavatory down the hall. He returns.

A muffled buzzer in the distance, down the hall. A flash of blue as the porter dashes by. Robinson marks haphazardly on a memorandum in red, a distasteful typographical error.

A click and muffled conversation. Another flash of blue as the porter returns.

Robinson rubs his eyes. Flatulence from somewhere ahead of him drifts by, and he wrinkles his nose. And rubs his eyes.

***

Robinson's eyes shot open at the muffled sound of something pounding lightly in the vestibule. Bringing his hand up to rub away the grogginess, he realized he was on the verge of falling asleep. The sound that had stirred him was gone, so he set about determining the particulars of his situation. His watch told him the time was 2:13 in the morning. The scene outside his window—to wit, blackness—told him nothing. He considered summoning Lucius to obtain an update, but ultimately decided to investigate on his own.

Rising, he exited his section and turned right, toward the observation car. It would be deserted this time of night, and he might be able to make out the train's location from the lights at the rear of the car. Passing through the vestibule, he felt a burst of cold air. He paused momentarily, figuring that a seal was loose somewhere around him, but the feeling of cold dissipated rapidly. He noticed wetness on the metal floor of the crossover plate between the cars. Yes, a loose seal. He would see to it when next saw Lucius.

Moving on, he entered the dimly-lit lounge. It was, as he expected, empty, save for what seemed to be a pile of coats in one of the seats. This struck him as curious and, as he approached, the pile resolved itself into something else entirely: a body.

It was male, and lay slumped on the chair with its arms splayed. The head was tilted back at an unnatural angle, and the skin was pale. Robinson knew there was no life left in it by the eyes alone. Even if he hadn't, both the dagger protruding from its sternum and the red pool of blood that had gathered at the naval of the grey jacket would have provided sufficient evidence. He squinted; it was the man he had seen talking with Brummell in the lounge only hours earlier.

The train was motionless, and the snow piled higher outside. Grafton was still miles away, and no help would be available for at least several hours. The railroad policeman knew what had to come next.

Confirming the lounge was otherwise empty, he dashed back to his room to summon a conductor, a porter, and to grab his gloves. Lucius appeared quickly, and Robinson had him retrieve the railroad's conductor, Mr. Preston, before drawing them both into the lounge with instructions to observe, record what he was told, and remain quiet. His witnesses secured, he proceeded to canvas the body.

The ostensible cause of death was the dagger. Sprouting from the corpse was a handle inlaid with onyx and mother-of-pearl, its blade buried deep near the man's heart. A glyph decorated its side, with a mirror image on the reverse. "An 'M'," Robinson said, "or is it an 'E'? This is too highly stylized for me to tell." Grasping with the thumb and forefinger of his gloved right hand, he tugged on it as slightly as possible to draw it back. "This is not a dagger." Robinson said, as much to himself as to Lucius. "It is a letter opener. A very fine one." He paused, leaving the bloody blade exposed half-an-inch but otherwise secure where it was found.

"Someone stabbed him with a letter-opener? And killed him?" Preston exclaimed.

"A sharp letter opener driven properly into the body can kill, yes," Robinson said absently, his attention focused elsewhere.

The victim's right hand, hanging limply over the arm of the chair, was open and empty. His left, however, was clinched into a fist. Prying open two of its fingers, Robinson found a small silver chain, likely a watch chain, though no watch seemed to be attached. He did not remove it, but logged this fact with Lucius, who dutifully wrote it down. The man's double-breasted grey suit jacket was unbuttoned, and Robinson first searched its outer pockets. In the small ticket pocket on the right, he drew out a collection of railway tickets and set them aside. The large outer pockets yielded a scratch pad with most of the pages torn out, a large matchbook bent back to allow easy access to its contents, and, hiding so effectively at the bottom of the pocket's well that he almost missed it, a small tube of red lipstick. "Curious," Robinson remarked as showed the tube to the other men.

Flipping the jacket open, he searched the interior pockets. Here, he found a wallet and a U.S. passport in the right pocket, both preserved from the blood still seeping into the cloth. Flipping the passport open, he saw it belonged to the dead man, one Paul Schmitt. Lucius logged all of these things while Preston stood awestruck by the event, frequently shaking his head and muttering softly to himself "On my train. On my train."

The left pocket was soaked through with blood. Feeling it gently, Robinson could feel something within. He gingerly removed what he discovered to be a B&O brochure advertising the wonders of a visit to the national capital, a large silver cigarette case, a cigarette lighter, and a small book of matches that, though closed, was clearly almost depleted. Its front advertised the Pennsylvania Hotel of New York City. Looking to the nearest ashtray, Robinson found a single snuffed-out cigarette, barely smoked, with a long, used matchstick laid beside it. The other trays were empty, cleaned out by the attendant when the car closed for the night.

Robinson first considered the brochure. Such advertising booklets were extremely common on the B&O, and Robinson could recite this one's contents almost from memory. When the last of the free-flowing blood had dripped off of it, Robinson placed it atop a handkerchief on a side table. He then turned over the bloody cigarette case and, finding nothing of interest, flipped it open, finding only a large quantity of cigarettes. No wonder he carried two matchbooks and a lighter, Robinson thought.

His search of the pockets complete, Robinson pulled the jacket back further and froze as he saw a holster. Inside it was a pistol, what appeared to be a semi-automatic Mauser. The holster was buttoned and the pistol was undisturbed.

"It seems Mr. Schmitt felt he needed protection in his travels." He said dryly.

"For what good it done him," Lucius finished *sotto voce.*

Robinson expanded his search to the rest of the lounge. Finding nothing out of place, he repaired to the bar area. The small kitchen was locked, but there seemed to be a moist spot on the floor. Crouching down, Robinson found several small, green glass shards swept under the edge of a cabinet. Robinson said nothing, but rose and addressed himself to the conductor, asking if the train had made any stops between where it presently stood and the station at Keyser. Preston replying in the negative, Robinson quickly darted to the solarium windows and squinted. Satisfied with what he saw, he returned to his companions.

"Gentlemen," Robinson began, addressing his witnesses, "we have here a murder. Until the authorities arrive from Grafton—please notify them as soon as possible, Mr. Preston—

the scene of the crime is in my custody. My intention is to begin an investigation at once, cognizant of the fact that the murderer of Mr. Schmitt is still aboard this train."

"What?" Preston exclaimed. "How do you know?"

"There are no footprints leading back down the track. He could not have escaped by going forward, for the engineers would have seen him. He could not have escaped to the train's port or starboard because we are at rest on the side of a steep hill." He paused, turning to look out the rear of the carriage. "The ground levels out behind us, but he would still have to retrace our path for an eighth, maybe a quarter of a mile before being able to make an escape."

He exhaled, and cast his eye down to the corpse. "Besides, even if he could get off the train, he is in the middle of nowhere in the midst of a blizzard. Although we could, of course, be dealing with a madman or a naïf, I somehow doubt he is that mad or idiotic to become, just that like that," he snapped his fingers, "an experienced mountain man capable of taking to the hills. No, gentleman, we have a murder to solve." He looked up, at his colleagues, "And let us pray that we need not use the plural before we catch him."

Lucius and Preston nodded somberly. Robinson checked his watch.

"It is 2:30. The passengers will not wake for some time. Lucius, speak to the porter in the sleeper beyond the *Loch Awe* and then lock the door between them. No one in, no one out. Then, station yourself between our car and the observation. As the passengers riding to the rear of my section rise, bring them to me here, one by one."

"Why the *Loch Awe*? And why to the rear of your section?" Preston asked. "Couldn't the murderer be anywhere on the train?"

"No," Robinson replied. "I was working in my section from Keyser until I discovered the body. No one passed by my room in the corridor, so the murderer must have been in either the sleeping compartments of the observation car or those accommodations in the Loch Awe between my section and the vestibule." Grabbing some stationery from a nearby table, he sketched out a rough diagram of the situation; Preston and Lucius helped him fill in the details.

"That's all right," Preston concluded as he finished. "But, Mr. Robinson, what about the body? We can't have you interviewing people right by the corpse. Can we?"

"You're correct, of course. Gentlemen, find us a few blankets and some tape. We'll drape and hang them until we've secluded the lounge from the dinette. The smell…well, we'll crack open a window once we've cordoned off the lounge."

The other men nodded and began to break away to see to their tasks. "Lucius, wait," Robinson called out. "I must first get some notion of who the victim is. After you speak to your colleague in the next carriage, bring me Mr. Brummell."

Lucius nodded, trusting in the judgment of the veteran policeman. "Will do, Mr. Ellicott."

Alone again with the deceased, Robinson reflected on the eerie stillness of the scene. No music of steel-upon-steel. No horn. No conversation or aromas to enliven. Merely stillness. Soon, as the window came down and the interviews began, an icy coldness would descend.

Traversing his eyes from Schimtt's unnatural pose to the small pile of evidence he had assembled on the dinette, Robinson remarked plainly, "Now it begins."

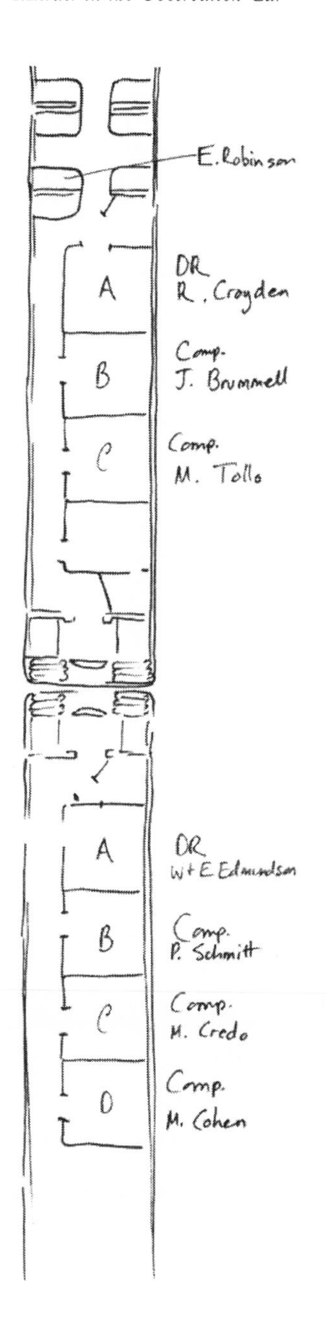
E. Robinson
A
DR
R. Croyden
B
Comp.
J. Brummell
C
Comp.
M. Tollo
A
DR
W+E Edmundson
B
Comp.
P. Schmitt
C
Comp.
M. Credo
D
Comp.
M. Cohen

CHAPTER EIGHT

Robinson and Preston were busy while Lucius attended to his tasks. Working with materials ready at hand, they devised a crude curtain of Pullman-branded blankets to conceal the body. With the barrier in place, they cracked a window near the corpse, and the car was gradually growing colder.

Robinson suppressed a shiver as he dismissed Preston. Alone for a moment in the lounge, he contemplated the crime. A passenger murdered, likely in the middle of the night, in an empty observation car on one of the premier passenger trains in America. Nothing but a blizzard and an equally inhospitable wilderness outside. No known motive—either for the murder or for the presence of the victim in the lounge—and no known leads as to suspicious passengers, lurking personages, or mysterious footprints. Robinson sighed heavily as he prepared for the work ahead.

He hated the cold, and its intrusion into the normally warm and refined and *civilized* space of the observation car offended him. He sniffed, a slight gesture of indignation directed at the circumstances of the evening. The B&O's honor was at stake, to say nothing of his own. He would solve this case, and quickly.

The train would resume. He would see to it.

Approaching the dinette table he intended to use for the interviews—the same table, in fact, at which he had eaten only hours before—he removed a small notebook and his watch from his pockets. The watch, placed authoritatively on the table for reference, stood at 2:57. Seating himself, Robinson positioned his notebook along with a pen in front of him, steepled his fingers, and waited. It was only a moment later when Lucius entered with Brummell, clothed hastily in a dressing gown, in tow. The young man looked unsteady, confused, and more than a little perturbed.

"Mr. Robinson," Brummell began, "what's going on? The train's stopped, have we derailed? What's so urgent?"

Motioning for him to sit, Robinson shook his head. "I'm afraid it's much more complicated than that." Dismissing Lucius with a grateful nod, he sized up the diplomat. Confusion was evident on his face, though the absence of dark circles under his eyes suggested he had been sleeping when Lucius had found him. He seemed curious and concerned, but showed no outward signs of anxiety. He shivered slightly as he approached the table, the cold air easily cutting through his thin robe.

"More complicated than a derailment?" he asked as he sat.

"Yes, indeed," Robinson replied. "The train is presently stopped by an obstruction ahead. But that's not why we need to talk. Instead, I've asked you here to talk about the gentleman in the grey suit—the one you were conversing with this evening in this carriage and, earlier, in the club car."

Brummell's brow furrowed. "Yes, Paul Schmitt. What about him?"

"He is behind me, on the other side of that partition. Murdered." Robinson scrutinized his face closely, using the shocking word like a prod to detect honesty. Brummell did not disappoint: his jaw dropped, briefly but genuinely, before a more measured, composed expression followed. Robinson expected this from a diplomat, which seemed to confirm at least that part of Brummell's story.

"Good Lord! How?" He paused, his eyes darting to the curtain. "*Why*?"

"Stabbed with a letter opener for the former. As for the latter, that's what I intend to find out. We are stranded miles from civilization. The conductor tells me that the snow has precipitated a small rock slide ahead of us. It will be cleared soon, but for now I must move quickly to locate the murderer." A brief explanation of his thinking followed.

"That makes sense," Brummell judged. "But why would someone murder a man under these conditions? There's nowhere to run, a limited number of realistic suspects since we all share the same corridor to move about…" He trailed off before finishing, "It makes no sense."

"Perhaps, but it's my job to find the reason in the madness. And I want you to help me begin this task," Robinson concluded.

"Why me?"

"You seemed on comparatively intimate terms with Mr. Schmitt. You are also a government employee, and, in my judgment, an intelligent one."

"But…how…how do you know I'm not the murderer?" Brummell seemed awestruck.

"I do not *know*. But I do doubt that conclusion. In part because you are too likely a suspect."

"Wait, too *likely*?"

"We'll come to that point later."

"So…I'm the prime suspect?"

"For a lesser investigator, perhaps." He sniffed. "In any event, I *must* begin with you since you have a relationship with the suspect and I am bereft of any investigative resources. Rest assured, I *will* be watching you. But, for now, I simply wish to know what you know. Begin by explaining to me how you knew Schmitt."

Brummell cleared his throat and began to relate the events of the last twenty-four hours. Robinson felt his eyebrows involuntarily lifting as the younger man described his chance meeting with Schmitt on the *Constitution*; he looked down and scribbled on the notepad before him to hide his intense interest. Brummell proceeded to recount their brief encounter in the baggage-lounge and, finally, their conversation in the observation car. This most recent meeting, as he told it, was uniformly anodyne, touching upon such commonplace subjects as foreign policy, trains, and cuisine.

"And then I came right out on the platform with you at Keyser. Remember—we saw that steam engine roll by—and the tribulations of the Pullman men? And then, to bed for the night," he concluded.

Robinson paused, placing his pencil on the table, addressing his gaze to Brummell's eyes, and forming his fingers into a pyramid before him. An awkward silence ensued as the railroad man evaluated his subject. He noted particularly that Brummell had not mentioned seeing Schmitt on the platform at Keyser, but, given that the latter had walked in the other direction, he allowed for the possibility that Brummell had indeed not seen the other man.

After a time, he broke his pyramid, dropped his gaze, retrieved his pencil, and spoke in a methodical monotone, his words as much for himself as his interlocutor.

"The deceased travelled with you from New York to Washington on business, yes?" Brummell responded affirmatively. "You rode together on the Pennsylvania's *Constitution* to

Washington, and not on one of the B&O's trains. You rode it because you arrived late into New York and had an early meeting the next day at the State Department. Why did Mr. Schmitt make the same choice? What business did he have in Washington?"

"He didn't say exactly," Brummell responded. "He mentioned that he had clients there, I believe."

Robinson shook his head vigorously, and emotion crept back into his tone. "And yet he told you nothing of the particulars of his business. Only that he traveled frequently, and usually by train." It was a statement, not a question, and Robinson continued, "There is something not right with this..." An idea occurred to him, "Did he say that he had been in New York for business, or was he just passing through?"

"He said he had been in New York for a few days." Brummell sounded intrigued.

Robinson sprang from his seat and retrieved the railway tickets he had taken off the corpse. Laying them out on the table, he said softly, "Six tickets." Three railway tickets sat beside three Pullman berth tickets.

"Six tickets," Brummell repeated in a similar tone. He paused, shook his head as though emerging from a trance, and said hesitantly, "Six tickets?"

"Observe," Robinson responded, pointing to the first pair. "There are three pairs of tickets, each pair representing one railway journey on a particular train—the railway tickets—and a particular accommodation—the Pullman tickets. See here this first pair: New York to Philadelphia. One ticket for the Pennsylvania Railroad, one for a Pullman parlor car seat. This is the journey you took yesterday."

Brummell's eyes lit up, "But Schmitt traveled to Washington, not Philadelphia."

"Exactly. See the second pair: Philadelphia to Washington.

Same railroad. Same date. Same parlor seat."

Brummell looked confused. "But why would he purchase two separate legs on the same train?"

"Why indeed..." Robinson was thinking once more, and silence again reigned. Using his middle finger, he slowly scooted one of the tickets in a circular motion on the table. "Ah. See here," he said gesturing to the Philadelphia to Washington Pullman ticket, "the handwriting is different on the two Pullman tickets. These were sold to him by different people, which most likely means at different times." He flipped both over and discovered an agent's stamp on the New York to Philadelphia ticket, but the back of the second ticket was blank. "Very odd," Robinson remarked.

"Well...that's strange," Brummell offered limply. "Perhaps he considered staying over in Philadelphia for the night, but decided at the last minute to continue on to Washington instead? Rather than have a new ticket issued, he might have just purchased a separate leg."

"Perhaps." Robinson paused only briefly before continuing, "Finally, we come to the last pair, for his trip on the *National Limited* today. Both tickets are for Parkersburg."

"But he told me on the *Constitution* that he was travelling to St. Louis. He didn't say anything about going to Parkersburg."

"Yes," Robinson replied distantly. He flipped these over and discovered they were purchased only the previous night at Washington. "Mr. Schmitt seems to have been cavalier in his travel planning at every stage," Robinson said softly. He checked the pocket watch he had placed on the table. "Had we not been stopped by the snow, we would be only two hours from Parkersburg right now." He looked directly at Brummell. "He was only hours from escaping this fate."

Replacing his watch, he turned his full attention to Brummell.

"Yes. Now, to the evidence against you I passed over earlier: the victim was found holding a silver watch chain. I noticed in the baggage-lounge that you wore such a chain with your waistcoat. Yet, I also saw that you had moved your watch from your waistcoat to your breast pocket and attached it to a leather strap by time you spoke with Schmitt."

Alarm crossed his face. "Yes, that's right. I switched my watch to the leather strap and left my silver chain in my compartment before dinner. It's easier to access in tight spaces."

"That said, we should now repair to your bedroom and confirm my suspicion that your watch chain is indeed not where you believe it to be." The two suited action to words and moved quickly to Brummell's bedroom on the *Loch Awe*.

"I put it right here," the younger man said, opening his grip. He rooted around for a moment before looking up in shock. "The chain…it's gone."

"And you did not vend it or give it or in any way have Mr. Schmitt interact with it?" Robinson spoke in a low voice to avoid waking Brummell's neighbors.

"No, not at all."

"Did he comment on it at all? Pay any notice to it?"

"No, nothing." Brummell paused. "He wore a wristwatch. A large one." Another pause. "Yes, I remember that distinctly. On the *Constitution*. And—I saw him check it in the baggage-lounge earlier this evening."

"A wristwatch, you say?" Robinson paused, subconsciously drawing his right index finger over his mustache. "Strange that his corpse wore no watch at all."

"I'm certain. It was large, abnormally so, but seemed to fit with the persona his clothes were crafting for him."

Robinson jerked his head around sharply. "Explain exactly what you mean. Leave nothing out."

Brummell proceeded to recount in detail his initial observations of Schmitt's clothes and manner, concluding with his evaluation of the man's likely skill at whatever sales business it was he went about.

Robinson thought for a moment before speaking again. "Mr. Brummell, you have an amateur's gift for observation and analysis. I assume you have documentation that can confirm your employment with the United States Department of State?" The younger man reached into his grip and withdrew a thick folio of papers from which he selected several identifying documents.

"Very well," Robinson continued. "You will deputize for me for the time being, though you will obey my orders to the letter. Are we clear?"

"If that's what you want, Mr. Robinson. But, I'm no detective." His voice seemed unsure, trapped between excitement and dread.

"No matter. I am worth at least two detectives. Dress, and we'll make a search of Schmitt's compartment."

Robinson waited outside until James emerged, again attired in his suit. His waistcoat and jacket had not yet been buttoned, and his tie was shabby and crooked. "Prepare yourself, Mr. Brummell," Robinson said, reaching up to straighten his tie. He paused as he did so, as though momentarily fixated on something. "Is this a new shirt?" he asked.

"Um, yes," the other responded. "It's my backup. Right out of my grip. Why?"

"It has the look of having traveled," Robinson said judgmentally as he resumed his motion and continued, "We must look professional and ordered if our minds are to function in a like manner." He sized up his protégé. "Come, we don't have much time."

CHAPTER NINE

The detective and the diplomat entered Paul Schmitt's compartment with the greatest of care, careful to avoid disturbing any unexamined evidence and doubly careful to avoid alerting the other inmates of the *Capitol Escort*, any one of whom might be the murderer himself. The bed had been made up for the night but, though it bore some evidence of habitation, it had clearly not been slept in.

A search of Schmitt's limited luggage turned up the expected necessities of a train journey: a cheap novel, a small bag of candy, a box of matches, and various unremarkable articles of clothing. A locking attaché case was the only other item of interest. Robinson shook his head as he examined it and turned to Brummell, "Schmitt carried no keys."

"No matter," Brummell replied, "it looks to be unlocked."

Surprised, Robinson found the case opened easily. Inside were what they quickly determined to be business papers. Addressed to "Schmitt, Schmitt & Associates," they were alike in their references to planned meetings, deliveries of reports, and travel plans. Scrutinizing them, Brummell shook his head vigorously. "Mr. Robinson," he remarked, "don't you find it odd—"

"Yes," Robinson cut in, "the sum of this man's case of business papers reveals nothing at all about what he does for his business. Or even what field it might be in."

"A consultant?" Brummell offered helpfully.

"Perhaps." Robinson replaced the contents of the case and drew himself up. "Keep searching. But quietly."

A moment passed as the two men went over the compartment, often bumping into each other as they looked. Finally, Brummell accessed the small sink, finding in the process a small dopp kit of toiletries wedged awkwardly in its bowl. Picking it up, he remarked "Odd place for your dopp kit."

"Open it," Robinson commanded.

Inside was a collection of personal items for shaving and cleaning, all fit snugly into their own pockets. One item was not properly stowed: an unknown object wrapped in a wash cloth. Robinson unwrapped it, revealing a large, broken wristwatch. Its face had been smashed, and the casing of the mechanism was not sealed. It was stopped, its hands no longer connected to the dial, and the mechanical movement inside was still.

"That's his watch," Brummell confirmed. "An accident, perhaps?"

"What makes you say that?"

Brummell breathed in and exhaled before answering. "Well, if his—er, the murderer was the one to break it, why go to the trouble of hiding it so neatly here, where it's certain to be discovered?"

"Perhaps to inspire you to think exactly that: that the broken watch has no relationship to the crime."

"When, in fact, it does?" Brummell asked. "I don't know—maybe that's what the killer *wants* you to think. An, um, 'red herring', I think they're called." Robinson said nothing in return, but gestured for Brummell to keep searching.

Their efforts turned up no further items of interest, and the two men crept back to the observation car to review what they had learned. Robinson related briefly the possessions found during his canvass of the corpse, and declared his intention to list carefully the points of interest he had noticed.

"A man of uncertain business, but certainly *of* business," Robinson began, speaking of their subject. "And of business that might have required him to carry a weapon." At Brummell's surprised look, he added, "Yes, I forgot to mention: I found a Mauser on him. Unused."

He continued, "An attaché case left unlocked, and no keys in sight. A wristwatch, missing but later found smashed in his dopp kit. Duplicate train tickets. A small tube of lipstick, opened but barely used if used at all. A watch chain where it should not be. A letter opener where it most certainly should not be. Oh—and it was monogrammed. An 'M' or perhaps an 'E'."

"Who stabs someone with a personalized weapon?" Brummell asked, his statement not wholly sarcastic in case the detective was about to tell him that this was indeed quite common.

"Yes, that is…well, odd," came Robinson's simple response.

"And the lipstick," Brummell continued, "what is it doing there? Perhaps it was planted, a clumsy attempt to suggest a woman was the murderer?"

"Perhaps." Robinson paused, grimacing. "To this list I must add a travel guide to Washington provided by the railroad."

"Why is that of interest?" Brummell asked.

"I didn't originally think it was…but the testimony of the Pullman tickets and your good self lead me in a different direction." Ignoring Brummell's look of confusion, he continued, "Finally: one other element, which I keep to myself for the time being." And then, ritualistically, "I have now enumerated the anomalous items that have volunteered themselves thus far." He snapped out of his reverie and addressed Brummell, "Besides, of course, the highly anomalous fact of murder on one of the B&O's very finest trains." Robinson offered a weak smile that Brummell found slightly deranged; still, he smiled back in an effort to be polite.

Robinson checked his watch and saw that it was fast approaching five o'clock. The train had yet to move. "We'll begin with Lucius."

***

Lucius the porter seemed ill at ease with the request to sit, so instead he stood for his interview with the railroad policeman and the overenthusiastic diplomat. Next to him stood Clide, the attendant for the observation car and a colleague of many years, and John, the waiter from the club car. Ellicott Robinson he knew—of course, most on the road did—and he trusted that his questions were friendly. The young Mr. Brummell he had only met yesterday, but he seemed the type that wanted porters to like him, which, in Lucius's experience, made a man not bad at all. He was not nervous at the inquiry, but rather astounded at its bizarre necessity.

"Gentlemen," Robinson began, "tell us if you please everything you know about Mr. Paul Schmitt."

Alas, the Pullman employees had little to add to his story; the two working the back of the train had spent most of their evenings forward—Lucius in the *Loch Awe* inventorying his supplies and Clide forward in the crew dormitory after closing the lounge around 11:00. Robinson made note of what information they were able to add: Schmitt's bunk had been put down around 9:00 while the gentleman was away. He had requested a wake-up shortly before his destination of Parkersburg, but only if he had not made himself known to the crew before that point. He seemed an amiable gentlemen who had engaged his fellow passengers in conversation; Lucius volunteered that he seen Mr. Schmitt speaking briefly to the naval officer outside the latter's bedroom before dinner, and Clide added that Mr. Schmitt had likewise spoken with the lady in black—a Mrs. Cohen—in the lounge shortly before Mr. Brummell arrived for his after-dinner appointment.

Finally, John added to Brummell's account by noting Schmitt's club car conversation with a professorial figure in grey prior to his repast with the short, fat man in the loud suit—the end of which, Brummell noted, he himself had witnessed; John also reported overhearing snippets about President Truman and something about Italy as he passed the professor, but noticed nothing out of place.

"Very well," Robinson responded, checking his notes. "And did any of you gentlemen notice anything amiss or unusual to the rear of my own sleeping berth after the lounge closed at 11:30 last night?"

"Well," Lucius began, then paused. "The navy gentleman buzzed for me about 2:00, 2:05 this morning. He saw the train weren't moving, and wanted to know why. I told him and returned to my inventorying up front."

"Describe him for us."

"Well…" he drifted off, seemingly uncomfortable.

"Yes, I think I can guess," Brummell interrupted. Turning to Robinson, he continued, "Commander Tollo enjoys a tipple. Or several tipples."

"Ah, I see," Robinson replied, his mind flashing back to his own observation of the officer earlier that night. "Well, we'll pass over that for now." Lucius cast a grateful look at Brummell, who nodded respectfully in return. "Lucius, I saw you moving down the corridor a few times last night. When were you in the jump seat at the rear?"

"I was there filling out forms from about eleven o'clock to midnight, or roundabouts where we stopped. I talked with a few of the other porters and trainmen about the snow for a while, and that put me behind. Then I did my nightly inventory from about fifteen-till-one through to when the navy gentleman buzzed. I finished up my inventory and was getting a cup of coffee when you buzzed."

Robinson considered for a moment. "So, you were in no position to consistently observe the comings and goings from the *Loch Awe*'s first-class sleeping section to the *Capitol Escort* between midnight and two-thirty this morning, yes?" Lucius nodded in agreement, and Robinson dismissed the men.

Turning to Brummell, he remarked absentmindedly, "That's the window for our murder. And, as I suspected, that leaves us with suspects here in the *Capitol Escort* and in the *Loch Awe*'s rear third. I myself was working all through this period, and I saw no one other than Lucius head toward the rear, and he returned almost immediately."

"Presumably his meeting with the commander," Brummell offered.

"Yes. To whom we should probably now turn." He paused for a long while.

"Something the matter?"

"Yes. I mentioned that we should confine our search to the passengers behind my own section...but there was a noise I heard in the night. Stamping, I thought. It came from the vestibule." He sat his fist heavily on the table. "James," he said, using for the first time his opposite's Christian name, "when you came through to this car, did you notice a draft? Either time?" He looked intently at the other man.

"Um, no. No, I didn't. And when you first brought me in here, I was only in thin sleeping clothes and a robe…so I think I would've remembered a chill."

"Ah, but when I first entered—when I discovered the body—I felt a chill, if only for a moment. And there was moisture on the floor. Not a lot, but the remnants of water."

James fixed him with a stare. "You think someone came in from the outside, through the vestibule door. And maybe stamped feet to dislodge the snow."

"Perhaps."

"The murderer?"

"Perhaps." He slumped back in his chair. "Or perhaps not. The body seemed to have been dead for several minutes when I found it."

They sat in silence for a while until Robinson eyes narrowed. He uttered a barely-audible "perhaps" and then shook his head. "We should get on with the interviews."

He summoned Lucius, and instructed him to bring the naval officer in next. To Lucius's point that the officer had not yet appeared, Robinson responded, "No, he's awake. I heard him moving around while we searched Mr. Brummell's belongings. Anyway, I want to see him now."

Lucius withdrew, and Robinson turned to Brummell. "James, tell me quickly everything you know about this officer." James briefly related the details of his earlier encounter. Robinson's eyes flicked upward with insight at one point during his description, but quickly returned to their position of neutrality, staring unnoticing at a small blue demitasse of coffee Lucius has thoughtfully procured.

Lucius returned a moment later with Mario Tollo, his uniform disheveled and his olive complexion more green than it had seemed the previous night. He sat uneasily across from the investigators. Brummell greeted him and introduced the railroad detective; Tollo seemed to seize up at the mention of the policeman.

"Mr. Tollo," Robinson began, adopting a sympathetic tone in light on the other's obvious discomfort, "I'm sorry to trouble you, but I must tell you that we have a very unfortunate situation that must be dealt with immediately." Tollo's expression grew perhaps a shade greener. "There has been a murder on this train, right behind me in fact, of a Mr. Paul Schmitt. You might have met him?"

"Um. Uh, no. No, sir," he paused, swallowing, "I've not met any Mr. Schmitt."

"I see." Silence hung between them for a moment. "Perhaps you met him and did not realize…" His voice trailing off suggestively, Brummell stepped in to offer a description of Schmitt.

"Oh, yeah, well, yes," Tollo started, his eyes focusing on the table in front of him. "I did meet him once. In my cabin, right before dinner. I was going in to my room, and he stopped and stuck his head in. Wanted to know where we were." He looked up and continued, "I didn't—I don't anything about this part of the world." His expression was determined.

"So you did meet with him in your cabin, but only briefly," Robinson summarized flatly.

"Yes, that's right," Tollo confirmed.

Robinson shifted his eyes downward and scribbled something in his notebook. When he again met Tollo's gaze, his tone had softened appreciably. "My young friend here tells me you're in submarines. At Norfolk, I presume?"

"Yes, submarines, that's right. And I've been at Norfolk for a few months, working on a few things for intelligence. Hush-hush, of course." He paused, then added, "At sea before then."

Brummell shifted uncomfortably in his seat. The interview had clearly revealed one thing to him: gone was the gregarious, recruiting poster officer he had described to Robinson. In his place sat a taciturn, possibly ill but definitely frightened young man.

Robinson continued, "And what ship did you serve on prior to your posting at Norfolk?"

"The *Mingo*."

"Ah. You saw some action then?"

"During the war? Sure. Of course."

"And the *Mingo* was a fine ship?" Robinson fixed Tollo with a hard glance.

"Oh, she was indeed a fine ship. Terror of the Pacific, and then some." A smile. A bit of the dashing officer had crept back into his tone.

Robinson's expression suddenly changed as he switched lines of questioning. "The porter tells me you noticed the train had stopped and called for him around two o'clock."

Though it was not a question, Tollo volunteered a "Yes, that's right."

"And then you…went back to bed?" Robinson cast his eyes down to Tollo's trousers. "You've a bit of mud on your pants, by the way." His eyes strayed lower, to the scuff marks on the officer's black shoes.

Tollo's eyes widened slightly but he cast only a cursory glance downward. Instead, he trained his gaze directly on his interrogator and smiled. "Actually, I was mighty curious to see what was going on up front, what with the avalanche and all. So I hopped out through the vestibule and took a look."

Robinson nodded sympathetically. "Yes, of course. It really *is* something to see this sort of thing on the B&O." His nod became a warm smile. "You see this on those roads out west going through the Rockies sometimes, certainly, but we try to hold ourselves to a higher standard."

Tollo nodded in agreement, "Yes, of course." His tone suggested a gracious, broad-minded understanding of the railroad's embarrassment.

"It must have been quite a sight, I imagine." The warmth in Robinson's tone conveyed an invitation to describe. "Again, our grand blue diesel engines are not often at a standstill in the wilderness."

"Oh, absolutely. Those two big blue diesels facing off against a wall of snow! It was so cold, of course, that I jumped back inside. I must've mussed my trousers doing so."

Silence hung between the men for a moment a moment. "Finally, Commander, I need to ask if you have observed any odd or…suspicious behaviors among your fellow passengers. You understand, of course, this is merely a routine inquiry."

"Um. No, sir. I don't believe so. I've kept to myself, mostly." His head jerked slightly and he added, "Watching the scenery. That sort of thing."

Robinson exchanged a slight glance with Brummell, both wondering silently what scenery Tollo had been taking in amidst the dark of night and the blizzard.

"Perhaps…you took the time to write some letters," Brummell offered. "I'm sure a man like you has so many…relations he keeps up with via the mail."

"No. I'm not a letter writer, really." Tollo smiled, lupine beneath his clear disquiet. "The girls I meet in port I generally leave there."

"Well, I'm sure you have more friends than you realize—I remember seeing you at dinner," Brummell offered. "You were with a man in grey tweed. Studious. Flamboyant, in his way."

The question took him by surprise, but he quickly recovered.

"Oh. Yes. Professor Crayfish. Or something like that. A little weird, if you ask me. Studies art history or something. Maybe politics." He furrowed his brow. "Strong opinions about things I didn't know you could have strong opinions about." He looked up, obviously proud of his formulation.

Brummell cut in, "Did he say anything about the other passengers?"

Tollo thought for a minute, clearly struggling to recall. "Not exactly. Well, maybe." He looked directly at James. "He gestured to you and that stunner in red particularly. Said something about instinct and art, I think." He trailed off, then his gaze refocused. "Come to think of it, I saw her talking with your corpse right after boarding. The girl in red, I mean. Out in the corridor. I didn't hear anything, but it seemed like a private conversation, if you get my drift."

James opened his mouth to speak, but Robinson cut him off, "Yes, thank you for that, Commander. You were saying about your dinner companion's assessment of the crowd..."

"Right, I'm not sure what he meant—said something about the 'economy and aesthetics' of everyone onboard. To be honest, I didn't really follow. He said at dinner that you were all *boos-wah*."

Brummell shared a look with Robinson, and replied "I think you mean *bourgeois*, Commander. It's a term that means roughly 'middle-class'. A term used by Marxists, among others."

Tollo's eyes widened and his color rose. A distinct feeling of betrayal was conveyed. "Pinko!"

"Perhaps," Robinson interjected. "But we shall see. Thank you for your time, Commander." He clapped his notebook shut and pronounced the interview over. Tollo had risen to leave before Robinson stopped him, "Commander, one last measure. May I see your ticket check for your journey today? And your connection from Norfolk as well."

"My tickets? Sure, I suppose." He produced the *National Limited* tickets easily, but groped in his pockets for a moment before withdrawing a coach ticket from Norfolk to Washington. "I thought I might have thrown it out," Tollo explained. "I usually do."

Robinson examined each in turn, his eyes lingering over the ticket from the railroad that had carried Tollo to Washington. "I see you travelled from Norfolk via Richmond, arriving in Washington at 5:30." Tollo nodded, and Robinson continued, "Coach, Commander?"

"Yeah," Tollo responded, a flash of red coloring his sallow complexion. "What of it?"

Robinson handed the tickets back with a slight smile, a gesture of apology. "Nothing, nothing at all—I merely thought you might have taken a day section or a parlor seat to celebrate your journey."

"Can't have *too* much fun," Tollo mumbled as he retrieved his checks and set off for his cabin.

No sooner had Tollo withdrawn than Robinson turned to his companion, "He's lying."

"About what?" Brummell asked urgently. "Is he the murderer?" His eyes widened as he continued, "Did I not push him hard enough on the letter opener—his name has an 'M', after all?"

Robinson, in no mood to be goaded, replied simply, "Never mind on the first point. As for the second, we have more work to do before we can know." He flipped his notebook back open as he continued, "As for the third, I don't think pushing him further would have yielded anything." Returning his attention to Brummell momentarily, he explained: "Somehow, I don't see him as the type to carry a letter opener with him on a journey."

He sniffed slightly. "Nor a book, nor any of the rudiments of civilization beyond the hip flask."

Seeing Lucius returning, Robinson requested that he rouse the professorial figure in the *Loch Awe*'s drawing room A.

"I imagine we have some time before Lucius can compel his attendance," Robinson declared as Lucius departed. "James, come with me and help me think." The two men walked over to the side table where the contents of Schmitt's pockets were laid out. Their reflections likewise assembled before them in the window behind the table, ghostly figures in green and blue.

The tickets they had gone over earlier were off to one side, while the other articles sat clustered together. Robinson gestured to the small book of matches and remarked, "It seems he stayed at the Pennsylvania before boarding your train."

"Logical," James replied, "given that it's right next to the station and he was known to travel."

As he spoke, Robinson picked up the larger matchbook that was folded over. "Odd that he would use two matchbooks simultaneously," he remarked, eyes narrowing. "Especially when travelling with a large box of his own along with a lighter." He ran his thumb over the remaining matches. "This book is larger than the other," he noted. He flipped the cover forward with his thumb, closing the book and revealing cover artwork of the Cunard Line's *Queen Mary*.

"That's the ship I was on!" James exclaimed upon seeing it. Looking closer, he added, "In fact, I remember giving him a light on the train from New York." He looked over at Robinson. "Maybe he pocketed it there. I think I just left it on the table."

"You just *abandon* matchbooks as a matter of routine?"

"Well, no. I…I tend to accumulate a lot of ephemera when I travel. Matchbooks, stationery, souvenirs…that sort of thing." His hand went to his right vest pocket and he withdrew a stash of matchbooks from the Willard Hotel. "It's the pack-rat in me, I suppose."

"Hmph," Robinson replied with a hint of disapproval at the carelessness which had now entangled Brummell even more tightly with the murder. "Why would he ask for a light when he carried his own lighter—to say nothing of the matches we've found?"

"Maybe it was out of fuel?" Brummell offered.

"Hmph," Robinson's reply again conveyed no confidence. Suddenly in motion, he crossed through the flimsy barrier concealing the back of the car. There, he examined once more the ashtray with the barely-smoked cigarette. The remnants of a match lay beside it. "You're sure he wasn't on your sailing?" Robinson called back to Brummell as he looked.

Still by the table of evidence, Brummell picked up and fingered the man's passport, "This passport would tell us if he was."

Robinson reappeared through the barrier. "There is a single cigarette in the ashtray beside him. And a match, long, like those from the *Queen Mary* book…"

"No," Brummell answered, anticipating the question in the other's trailing voice, "I have no idea how a match from one of my books ended up beside his body."

"Check his passport," Robinson instructed.

Flipping through it, Brummell shook his head. "There's nothing here. Not just no trip on the *Queen Mary*, mind you—no visas at all. No record of entries or exits. No real evidence of use." He turned his head to Robinson. "Why would he bother with a passport at all if he doesn't travel abroad?" In the window, his reflection's hands subconsciously turned the passport over and over as he pondered, the blurry blue suit merging with the blue cover of the passport.

"Perhaps he intended to do so in the near future?" Robinson offered.

"The issue date is 1946," Brummell replied. "So it doesn't appear so."

A pause descended as both men contemplated. "Something feels wrong here," Robinson finally declared.

"Yes, something does…feel…wrong." Brummell's hands had stopped. "Something *does* feel wrong." He flipped it open and felt the back cover. "This feels too thick."

Robinson took the passport and felt for himself. "You're right." The green and blue reflections huddled together over the passport. Retrieving a pocket knife, he sat it down and slid the knife's blade along its interior spine. Then, feeling inside his incision, he withdrew a thin piece of flimsy paper, folded and fit tightly into the passport's back cover.

He unfolded it, revealing a photo of Schmitt's head accompanied by a page of almost translucent writing in red. The script was unreadable, save for four characters arranged recognizably at the top: *CCCP*. "The U.S.S.R.," James said in wonder. "He's a Soviet!"

"Yes," Robinson responded in a more measured tone, "clearly Mr. Schmitt had depths we have not yet plumbed." He sat both documents down, slowly shaking his head. Casting irony aside, he muttered a curse he had picked up from an old friend, "*Sacré*!"

Conscious of the gravity of the situation, James resisted the urge to smile.

"I don't suppose reading Cyrillic script is among your many skills?" Robinson asked hopefully.

"Alas," Brummell responded, frustration evident in his voice.

"No matter. This casts quite a different light on our

investigation nonetheless."

"He did seem very interested in international affairs when we spoke…I guess this goes a long way toward explaining that."

"Perhaps," Robinson mumbled, deep in thought. Turning his attention to Brummell, he asked, "But he never asked you to reveal anything confidential?"

"No," the younger man replied, "not at all. His questions were entirely innocuous—mostly the same sort of thing I'm asked all the time by people from all walks of life, just put in a more sophisticated framing." He paused, considering. "He did have one or two insights that were uncommon. But I chalked that up to him simply reading between the lines of newspapers." He looked directly at Robinson. "Nothing untoward or illicit passed between us, certainly. And I never had the feeling that I was being probed for information beyond the bounds of propriety. Or even normality, given the headlines you see these days."

Robinson's voice was somber. "Yes, the situation in Berlin. It seems we all have a stake in it. We all have an interest."

Noise in the corridor signaled the arrival of their next passenger. Robinson instructed James to say nothing of their latest revelation as the two made their way back to the table.

CHAPTER TEN

Professor Robert Croyden lumbered to the table, a scowl on his face the first thing noticeable about him, outdoing even his prominent mustache, ice-blue eyes, and large spectacles. Clearly in his mid-50s, with a shock of white hair and a physique that bespoke a sedentary lifestyle of books and talk, he sat with an audible grunt before starkly beginning, "What is the meaning of this? I was soundly asleep!"

"Sir, a murder has been committed on this train," Robinson replied sharply, his voice taking on the air of a *maître d'hôtel* indignant at a guest's complaint that his duck was undercooked. Brummell struggled to keep surprise off his face as the older man continued in a prim, patrician tone that he had not used previously. "I, a railroad detective, have assumed direction of this situation and, as a part of my investigation, I require a few minutes of your time. Since we are snowbound for the moment and must wait for the local police to begin their work, I trust I'm not overly inconveniencing you by starting early and speeding the process along."

The other man cocked an eyebrow at the discourse emerging from the mouth of the humble railroad detective, shrugged slightly, scowled deeply, and surrendered to the tide of events. "A murder. Horrendous." His tone implied distaste, but also disinterest.

When nothing else emerged from him, Brummell stepped in to offer proper introductions for himself and Robinson. When he had finished, Croyden asked snidely, "And what gives *you* standing to assist our detective here with his little inquisition?"

Refusing to rise to the bait, Brummell answered evenly, "As an officer of the United States government and an acquaintance of the deceased, I'm here to provide whatever assistance I can to Mr. Robinson."

"Indeed, sir," Robinson said, jumping in. "Mr. Brummell and I undertake a difficult task. You see, we believe the murderer to still be with us. Here, on this train."

Croyden drew back slightly, his eyes widening. The situation seemed to interest him marginally more than before. "Well then, get on with it! I've no desire to be murdered in my berth—though, were I to be so, I'd hope that *real* policemen would be in charge of the investigation." He sighed heavily and continued, "What are your questions?"

Robinson exhaled slightly before continuing, the only sign that he understood or acknowledged the insult that had been hurled at him. "First, please enlighten us as to your name, itinerary, and purpose for travelling—where do you come from, where do you go," he trailed off, a meaningful pause, "what do you do?"

"My name is Robert Croyden. Professor Robert Croyden."

"I'm sorry, Professor," Robinson cut in, his pencil poised at his notebook, "but could you perhaps add your middle name? For my records."

"Fine. Robert *Edward* Croyden. I…I am a tenured professor of political science on long-term leave from my university," he stammered. Brummell sensed he had been put on his back-foot, but was unsure quite why. "I am travelling from my home in Baltimore to St. Louis, where I intend to stay for the next few months, writing and thinking." The formality and rigidity of his tone seemed both rehearsed and deeply uncomfortable.

"May I examine your ticket checks?" Robinson asked. Croyden produced three specimens: a coach ticket from Baltimore on the *National Limited*'s southward leg from New York to Washington, and two tickets covering the Pullman accommodation to which he had switched when the car had been added at Washington. Robinson inspected the connecting ticket and set it aside, his attention lingering for a moment on the two tickets for the journey westward. The Pullman check matched his berth in a full drawing room in the *Loch Awe*.

"I see you came from Baltimore to Washington on this train's first leg. When the train was reassembled and expanded for its run west, you moved from a day coach to the Pullman, then?" Robinson said absentmindedly.

"Yes," Croyden responded before adding sarcastically, "It heartens me *so* to know that a railroad policeman can read a ticket."

"Why not simply book Pullman accommodation for the whole journey?" Robinson countered, ignoring the barb. "I believe there was through space available."

Croyden blasted air through his nostrils in a sign of dismissal. "And pay the extra fare for an hour's jaunt to Washington? What's the use? Besides, I'd have to change carriages at Washington anyway to move into a proper drawing room for the night."

Robinson returned the tickets and conceded the point, "Perhaps you're right." Then, he suddenly switched tones and prodded his disagreeable interviewee, "And your university?"

"Carroll University. In Maryland." The response was tight-lipped. No barbs or elaboration trailed his words.

"And your reason for taking leave?"

A long pause intruded before Croyden responded. "I won't trouble you by either lying or delving into unnecessary detail. It was felt that some time away from campus would benefit all involved. I trust you will leave it at that."

A burst of intuition caused Brummell to suddenly interject, "A scandal of some sort, professor? A scandal…over politics? Over Marxism, perhaps?"

His reply came rapidly, words overlapping as his face reddened. "Scandal! Politics! Why, what do you know about socialism, you little whelp! Do you think I—a man of *my stature* would be a grubby little socialist?"

"Your stature?" Robinson interjected. "What do you mean, Professor?"

His lips quivered a moment before answering, as though he were turning over a question in his mind. "I am not *just* a professor—I am consulted by some very important people in Washington." He fixed Brummell with a glare, "I've even met your boss, once or twice."

"And so…" Robinson began flatly, "you are *not* a communist?" His brow furrowed slightly as though in confusion.

Croyden's eyes widened and his face resumed its burgundy hew, but he caught himself before firing back. His nostrils flared as he calmed himself and replied, "No. I am *not* a communist. My leave of absence is down to a personal matter. An affair of the heart."

The invocation of such a personal concern seemed to throw Robinson off the scent, and the confusion evident on his face just before seemed to evaporate. "Ah, I understand completely, sir. To other matters, then." He flipped through his notebook for a moment before asking about his relationship to the deceased.

"Yes, the slicked-back salesman in the *au courant* suit. We sat near one another in the club car early in the journey. We spoke of nothing of consequence."

"Is that so?" Robinson replied. "I would imagine that, when speaking with a man as knowledgeable and…*consequential* as yourself, there would be no end to the fascinating topics to discuss. Why, our naval companion mentioned that your conversation at dinner ranged widely, covering art, fashion…politics…"

"Oh yes, I'm happy to prattle on in unintelligible terms about things far above the comprehension of the plebs that trouble me on trains and buses and so on." He sniffled slightly. "It provides me with a measure of entertainment on long journeys."

Ignoring the provocative, aggressive tone of the older man, Brummell interjected, "And did Mr. Schmitt provide you with an avenue for such…entertainments?"

"I believe we talked about Truman's defense cuts. And about which Italian beaches provide the best opportunities for dissolution." He sat back, a self-satisfied look upon his face. "I doubt he understood a lick of either topic. Frankly, I felt the urge to tell him to stick to brushes or dry goods or whatever product with which he troubles himself as he goes door to door." His voice dripped with condescension.

Brummell laughed softly, attempting to build a rapport. "You know, I had a similar thought when I met Mr. Schmitt—about what he did for a living, I mean. Did he really sell dry goods?"

Croyden's face went limp in disbelief, "How would I know—or care?"

Robinson broke his silence, "You have travelled, perhaps, to Italy?"

"I have travelled extensively," he flatly replied.

Silence hung between them for a moment before Robinson continued, "I'm sure you often write to your friends to tell them about your adventures. Did you perhaps meet any interesting people on the train last night—characters to fill the pages of your letters?"

"As you may have already gathered, I'm not terribly interested in any of you. Had I correspondents intriguing enough to write," he said, leaning in with a sneer, "I doubt any of you would be interesting enough to make the final draft."

Robinson refused to be baited. "Come now, Professor. I saw you engaged in quite lively conversation with the young lady dressed in black last night."

"Ah. Her. Pretty, but sharp. Cold. We discussed calligraphy, which she does a bit of, and art." He blinked. "She offered no new insights on either."

"And, on the subject of the deceased, did you speak with any of the other passengers about him?"

"Hmmm," he paused. "Well, after dinner I had a mediocre orangeaid cocktail in the observation that would have been too weak for a septuagenarian nun. So, I took it forward to the compartment of my drunken dinner companion in hopes of finding something civilized with which to spike it. On my way there, I walked by that chorus girl your so-called diplomat here passed dinner with last night; she was standing in the observation corridor. Paused outside what I believe to be your dead man's compartment."

"And what time might that have been?" asked Robinson.

"Oh, say, 8:45. Maybe 9:00. Who cares on a train?"

"Funny that Commander Tollo didn't mention that you visited him," Brummell noted.

"Not at all funny, since he didn't answer his door." Croyden leaned in slightly and fixed them with a patronizing glare. "You see, I'm not sure our gallant salt was quite up to…well, anything at that moment. So I returned to my room and retired. And, with that, gentlemen, my role in your petty drama concludes." He rose from his seat.

"One last question, if I may," Robinson called after him as he turned to leave.

"What?"

"I was just wondering, professor, if you've published anything recently? A *magnum opus*, perhaps?"

Croyden paused, weighing his response, and spoke in an even tone, "I have not. Though I will. Soon."

Robinson crooked a corner of his mouth up, "Editors, eh?"

The other's expression turned sharp. "True artists have no editors," he replied, fixing Robinson with a glare. "Not in their art. And not in their lives." And with that, he was gone.

CHAPTER ELEVEN

The departure of the professor provided the investigators an opportunity to absorb all that had happened. They did so in a state of shared astonishment at the unpleasantness of the encounter.

"Tell me," James asked, "is there a correlation between misanthropy and murder?"

"If there is," Robinson sighed, "I believe we can stop here and now." Slight, weary laughter passed between the men.

"You caught his middle name, I assume."

"Oh yes. Edward with an 'E'. I'd expect James *Matthew with an 'M'* Brummell to notice that," Robinson said evenly.

"I was wondering if you had picked up on that from my file, since you hadn't asked me, *Ellicott*," Brummell replied, choosing to take it with a smile. "But you didn't mention the letter opener to Croyden directly."

"No. His declamation on the subject of letter-writing ensured that he would deny owning such a thing whether or not it was his anyway." Under Brummell's searching gaze, he continued, "The guilty will lie because they are guilty, and the arrogant will lie to defend their bluster."

"And the innocent?" Brummell countered.

"Well, we'll have to see," came Robinson's cryptic response.

That Lucius did not immediately appear indicated the other passengers were stirring, and an uneasy silence descended upon the car as the two men and one corpse waited for the next act in their little play.

The younger man, burning with questions, spoke first. "What was he lying about?"

"The Professor?" Robinson responded. "Oh, nothing that need concern you."

"No, the Comma—" Brummell broke off mid-sentence, his body jerking upright slightly as though he had been slapped. Plaintively, he continued, "Wait, the Professor was lying, too?"

"As I said, it is nothing material at this moment."

"Just like the Commander, I imagine. You still won't tell me what he was lying about?"

Robinson offered a slight shrug. "I don't want to muddy matters for you—or for him—until…well, until we gather more evidence to puzzle out."

A pregnant pause followed that was broken with Brummell's indignant declaration, "You don't trust me, do you Mr. Robinson?"

"Not wholly, no. One must be careful when cut off from the resources of the police. And civilization."

Brummell hung his head slightly and said more softly, "I'm still a suspect, aren't I?"

Running his fingers over his little mustache, Robinson demurred, "Come now, my boy. Of course you are! The only material evidence I have connects you to the victim. I must keep you in mind—no choice about it."

"So why have me participate in these little chats? Why give me access to the evidence?"

Now Robinson smiled, wide and genuine. "Good! You're thinking, now. I have you participate, perhaps, because I hope you might incriminate yourself." At Brummell's forlorn stare, he continued, "Perhaps, because I don't think you actually did it and think that your presence…your experiences, your mind…might prove…enlightening, in the end." Leaning back in his chair, he took his water glass and hungrily gulped its contents, a strange, unrestrained movement from one so clearly prim, proper, and controlled. Replacing the glass, he fixed his companion with a stare. "Besides, it's all much easier than tying up a porter to constantly watch you or embarking on the unlikely errand of imprisoning you in your compartment."

To his credit, Brummell offered a shaky smile at this last admission. "Yes, I suppose there is method in it."

Robinson nodded. "And for your recognition of this fact as much as for the Shakespeare reference, I'll grant one of your little wishes. Tell me, what struck you as odd about Professor Croyden's story?"

Brummell leaned slightly back, considering. "Well, for starters, his whole academic exile thing. 'Personal indiscretion' sounds to me like he made time with a co-ed. Frankly, it happens all the time. More than a few marriages come about that way, honestly. I've seen some myself." He reached up, feeling the stubble forming on his jawline. "Anyway, I've never heard of a college banishing a senior academic for it. At least when it was within the bounds of legality and propriety. The alternative is…something that would land him in a locale either a lot more remote or a lot less pleasant than St. Louis."

"Very good, James," replied Robinson warmly. "Yes, there is indeed something off about that."

"So why the banishment? Maybe something more sinister than he's letting on."

"Well, maybe. But maybe not. Perhaps he is telling enough of the truth that a little falsehood shouldn't deter us from taking his story seriously. Do you recall the name of his college?"

"Um. Carroll College. In Baltimore, I think. I'm not terribly familiar with it."

"Carroll College, my young friend, is an all-male school under the patronage of the Catholic Church."

"What does—ah." Brummell's eyes widened. "Ah."

"Ah," Robinson replied simply.

"Well, I guess I see how that fits."

"Precisely. But something else strikes me about this situation, and it encompasses both our fibbing professor and the truth of his story."

"Do tell," Brummell said in his best impression of someone not terribly excited by the whole process.

"I…*we* have now examined three of the potential candidates for the murder of what we now suspect to be a Soviet agent. Please enumerate them."

"Well," Brummell began, "we have our shifty sailor with the drinking problem fresh off of some intelligence assignment at Norfolk. We have a compromised professor of politics who boasts of his connections to the government." He paused, but only briefly. "And we have a bright, handsome, extraordinarily capable young diplomat just back from the high political fleshpots of Europe—a Europe always seemingly on the brink of war with the Soviet menace. That about sum it up?"

"Good, good," Robinson answered warmly. "You have indeed been keeping up. Yes, an unusual number of candidates that might be of interest to a spymaster. 'Loose lips sink ships', and so on."

"Of course, this train is heavily patronized by government employees, so you'd expect more than a few people blessed with high-level access to state secrets lurking about the Pullmans."

"Quite..."

"But..."

"Perhaps it is not mere coincidence." Robinson's voice trailed off, and he began muttering to himself, "This train. This train... these tickets for this train...this place..."

Robinson stood, motioning Brummell to follow, and walked to the table of evidence. "Two tickets, James. One to Philadelphia, another to Washington. On the same train. Purchased at different times."

"Yes, I recall. I thought we agreed he must have decided to extend his journey and simply purchased an extension rather than having the ticket reissued?"

"We decided no such thing!" Robinson passionately replied. "Two tickets, one train. Issued quite probably by different agents. He travels. He *plans* to travel. But *plans change*." He fixed Brummell with an intense stare. "Different agents...different *places*. James, you said Schmitt went early to dinner, dined with you, and that you finished dinner together just as the train reached Philadelphia, yes?"

"Yes, that's right."

"And yet Schmitt did not leave the train at Philadelphia?"

"No, he couldn't have. We were in the station as we left the dinette. He wouldn't have had time to gather his things and get off, surely. And he showed no hurry or sign of distress."

"Tell me," Robinson said slowly, "did he at any time leave your table for an extended period?"

Brummell paused, considering, "Yes. At Trenton—or thereabouts. He didn't say as much, but I assumed he needed the facilities."

Robinson remained silent for a moment, absentmindedly stroking his mustache.

"James," he began at last, "if Schmitt did indeed change his plans—plans that initially involved alighting in Philadelphia as late as the very day he boarded the *Constitution* but changed at some point to take him further south—then, wouldn't there be some residue of his initial scheme?"

"That's a logical assumption. A receipt, a reservation, a letter—something like that. But I didn't see anything of the type in his case. Nor anything that you pulled off his person."

Robinson paused, considering. "Then I must recanvas. This man may be a spy, but he is not a ghost. He must've left tracks, something that signaled his intentions."

Rising, he led the younger man past the crude partition that hid the corpse. There he stood in front of Schmitt's remains, clearly concentrating so hard that Brummell remained quiet, fearing to interrupt him.

"James," he said finally, "retrieve for me a towel from behind the bar." The younger man complied and, upon handing it over, witnessed the older man carefully wrap the towel around his hand. He then kneeled by the corpse and spoke. "In my initial search, I was at pains to avoid disturbing the site of the wound." His wrapped hand reached out, carefully entering the exterior breast pocket on the corpse's jacket, the one nearest his heart. "This entire area is soaked in blood. And I overlooked this particular pocket, probably out of a subconscious aversion to the fact that it is—" he cut off suddenly as his fingers grasped something. "Sorry," he apologized before continuing, "that it is saturated in blood. And that Mr. Schmitt lacked the good taste to wear a pocket square, the only sensible use of the exterior breast pocket."

Robinson turned to look at Brummell, grinning as he removed his hand, now containing several small slips of paper. "*Viola.* Lacking the sense of the sartorial that you and I, James, clearly share," he said as he rose, "Mr. Schmitt instead used his pocket for simple storage, a base choice indicative of his low character. Specifically, in this case, he used it for the storage of documents I believe he placed out of sight and out of mind. So far out of mind, in fact, that he forgot to dispose of them later."

The men moved to a side table. Brummell retrieved another towel and Robinson carefully sat the blood-soaked papers upon them and leaned down to examine. One was an unused Pullman ticket, another an equally-unused railway carriage ticket. "A pair for a journey not taken," Robinson suggested as he peered at them. The blood had smeared much of the ink, but the Pullman ticket—colored for a private bedroom—clearly showed a destination of Pittsburgh; its railway companion indicated it was for the Pennsylvania Railroad.

"Mr. Schmitt," Robinson declared, "was headed to Pittsburgh from Philadelphia. The date is smudged, but it was likely today." He looked up at Brummell but did not unfold himself, "This was his original itinerary."

"That would've been the most direct route to Pittsburgh. Something must have changed his plans and sent him to Parkersburg instead," Brummell offered.

Robinson returned his attention to the table and the thin sheet of carbon copy paper that lay alongside the tickets. The flimsy quality of the paper combined with the saturation provided by the blood rendered it all but unreadable.

"—e-g-r-a—" Robinson slowly spelled out, reading what little text was legible.

The older man suddenly snapped straight up. "It's a telegram receipt. He sent a telegram, and received this as a confirmation."

"But we can't tell anything else from it. Or even if it's connected."

"They may well be unrelated. But, psychologically, I think not. Why else pair these papers together in such an odd spot?"

"Perhaps he was going to submit them to the Kremlin as reimbursable expenses?" Brummell said with a gallows grin.

"You jest, but it could be as simple as that," Robinson said softly. "Anyway, we should be about our remaining interviews. Go forward and ask Lucius to bring us the young woman in mourning, Mrs. Cohen."

Brummell began to depart, but hesitated and turned back around. "What's that?" he asked, gesturing to the brochure Robinson had previously retrieved.

"It's a guide to Washington—an advertisement pamphlet produced by the railroad," Robinson answered. "After all, one of our mottos is 'All trains via Washington with stopover privilege'." Looking somewhat abashed, he added, "It helps us turn our very indirect routing into New York into a strength—'come and see the Capitol' and so on."

"Mr. Robinson, why would a Soviet spy be carrying such a guide? And why on a train heading out of the city?"

Robinson rocked back on his heels, considering. "James, you may have something there." His hand darted out and retrieved the brochure. Flipping through it rapidly, he encountered only familiar railroad copy before, toward the back, he saw something out of place. "Here, James, look."

There, pasted to the last pages of the pamphlet, was a flimsy piece of carbon paper with what appeared to be a key of some sort: numbers and letters array next to sequences, codes, words, and symbols. "Mr. Schmitt was not interested in the cherry blossoms, then?" James asked gravely.

"I think not, James," Robinson intoned. "I think not."

***

Mary Cohen knew how to make an entrance. The sun was only beginning its slow course over the horizon when she appeared, fully dressed, fully made-up, and fully stunning. The somber, matte blackness of her hat, her small veil, her dress, her gloves, her bag—it commanded the room with a standoffish seriousness, the undeniable, unavoidable authority of a beautiful woman attired for Serious Things. But the golden pillow of hair spilling out of the hat and gathered at the nape of her neck entranced where her clothing coerced, warmly seducing at precisely the moment her clothing declared her cold and distant and unfeeling. The paleness of her skin beneath the suntan, the redness of her lipstick, the quiet intensity of her green eyes—all came together in a palette that simultaneously repelled and attracted, but in both cases dominated.

Arriving at the threshold of the lounge, she paused long enough to remove a black cigarette holder and a short white cigarette from her long black clutch. That brief delay was all she needed, for the sun at the moment finally appeared and light, glinting off the pure white snowpack outside, poured into the narrow space of the lounge. The tableau complete, she cocked her chin slightly upward, revealing in the process her slender, elegant neck and the necklace of onyx stones that sat at its base. She moved forward, sitting in the proffered seat.

Inserting her cigarette into its holder, she dangled it slightly over the table. Brummell accepted the invitation, removing in the process one of his matchbooks from his waistcoat and lighting the cylinder himself. As he did so, Mary looked away, casting her glance out the windows across the aisle. The light had revealed the train to be on a hillside, and snow enveloped a valley below.

"A beautiful morning," the woman began as Brummell blew out the flaming match. She drew the holder to her lips and mildly inhaled. "However unfortunate the circumstances that find us looking out at it."

Brummell responded before Robinson could get a word out, his tone a notch deeper and more commanding than he had previously employed. "I suppose we've got to take beauty as we find it, where we find it. Don't you agree, Mrs….?"

Robinson arched an eyebrow at his companion's presumption but otherwise allowed the scene to play out.

"Cohen," the lady responded. "Mrs. Mary Cohen." She exhaled, smoke drifting from the right corner of her lips. Ignoring his question, she came right to the point. "The porter tells me you men are railroad police and you need to question me. He didn't say what, but his tone suggested it was something very, very serious."

"I am, indeed, a railroad detective, Mrs. Cohen," Robinson replied. "This is Mr. Brummell, a government employee who is acting as my second in this matter."

"And what matter might that be? Sabotage of the train in the middle of the West Virginia wilderness?" She spoke with a hint of weary ridicule on her breath.

"No, Mrs. Cohen," Brummell interjected, "this concerns the murder of one our fellow passengers. A Mr. Paul Schmitt, of… well, all over." He fixed his gaze on her eyes and, maintaining his deeper timbre, said simply, "His corpse rests behind this partition."

The news penetrated the young woman's carefully-curated demeanor. "A murder?" she exclaimed. "On a train?"

"I'm afraid so, Mrs. Cohen," Robinson said, attempting to regain control of the conversation and casting in the process a side glance at Brummell. "But we're getting ahead of ourselves. Please tell us about your reason for travelling today. And, if I may, accept our condolences for your loss."

His words hung heavy in the air for a moment before she replied, "I assume, detective, that you refer to my dress and not to your victim." Seeing Robinson prepare to interrupt, she pushed forward, "But I'm sure we'll talk about that in a moment—I've seen plenty of movies, so I have a sense of what's coming. No, gentlemen, I am in mourning for my husband." She paused for a moment, as though listening to herself. "I am a widow."

"May I ask how he died?" Robinson said softly.

"Overseas. Sick. Miserably," came her terse reply.

"May I assume you were with him at the time?" Robinson probed.

Again, a pause before she answered, her voice less steady than before, "No. I was on my way, though." She gnawed slightly at her holder before continuing, "He was in Africa. On business. He came down with something, and I was coming out to care for him. I got the news he was dead when my ship landed. Missed him by four hours." A long drag on her holder and an equally long exhaled interposed. "I settled his affairs there and returned home."

"And that is the reason you travel today? To return home?"

"Yes, to St. Louis. I arrived into Norfolk last week, and came up yesterday to catch this train."

"You'll forgive me for saying so, m'am, but your clothing is extremely fine. Do you travel with it often?"

"I gather, Mr. Inspector, the gist of your question," she said with bitterness seeping into her voice. "And, no, I do not. It took several weeks to settle my husband's accounts. My mother sent me proper mourning clothes in the interim."

"I meant no offence, m'am," Robinson replied. "May I ask as to the nature of your husband's work?"

"Business, as I said."

"What sort of business?"

"Import-export. Things of that nature."

"I see. You mentioned you travelled through Norfolk. May I see your tickets for this journey? And also the journey from Norfolk to Washington?"

She complied, producing from her bag the appropriate documents.

"You said you stayed in Norfolk for a week. You have family there, perhaps?"

"No. My husband and I kept an apartment there. I stopped over to clean it out."

"How very interesting," Robinson remarked noncommittally. "You know, my friend Mr. Brummell here works for the State Department. I wonder, James, if anything Mrs. Cohen just said might spark your interest. An international businessman splitting his time between Norfolk, an important port city, and—I'm sorry, Mrs. Cohen, what African nation did you say your husband was in?"

She exhaled through her teeth, "I didn't."

"Perhaps I might examine your passport, then." His response carried no hint of a question.

"Fine," she relented. Reaching into her bag, she continued, "It's Egypt. And, yes, my husband was involved in…government work. We…we were engaged while he was in college, and they recruited him right as he graduated. Right as we wed." She shook her head. "I'm not supposed to talk about it." Her eyes blinked rapidly, forestalling tears as her clipped, tight voice threatened to break. "The vainglory of those men, the vainglory they put into his head…sending him rushing off to serve the flag and…and, make me a widow." Her steel returned and she puffed on her holder. "It's not right."

Mystified, Brummell interjected, "Egypt…there's a lot going on there right now. A lot that interests the United States, and particularly the departments of State and Defense." He turned and spoke directly to Robinson, "We have quite a few pieces on that particular board right now. She shouldn't be talking to us about them."

Robinson considered, flipped through her passport, and slowly nodded. "Very well, Mrs. Cohen. Your husband passed away on government business in Egypt, and you return now to your home in St. Louis. Let's move on. You were on the Norfolk to Washington train via Richmond that arrived yesterday at 5:30, yes?"

"Yes, as my tickets plainly show."

"I understand that dashing naval officer was on the same train. Perhaps you spoke to him?"

"No, Mr...."

"Ah, Robinson. Ellicott Robinson, special inspector. Apologies."

"Right," the woman resumed, "I didn't see him on that train. I did see him yesterday evening, here in the lounge before dinner. He seemed to be having...a very good time. But we didn't speak." She turned her gaze to Brummell and continued, "The same can be said about you, minus the good time part. He was also in the lounge after dinner, but I only saw him leave so I must've had my back to him."

Brummell cleared his throat before replying, "Yes, I recall you were speaking with Miranda at the time. Before dinner, I mean."

"Miranda? Why, yes, I was."

"What did you talk about?"

"Well, Mr. Brummell, I don't see how that's entirely germane to this conversation." She clinched her holder between her teeth and spoke through them, "Though, if you must know, we spoke a little about you."

"Me? Whatever for?"

"Nice young man all alone in the lounge, keeping company with a recruiting poster gone bad? More interesting than the hills, I suppose. At least after the sun's gone down."

Robinson leaned forward, asserting control. "Perhaps we could discuss your relationship to the dead man, Mr. Schmitt?"

"Well, I didn't know him by that name and there *was* no relationship. I believe I spoke to him for a period here, in the observation car, last night. He introduced himself to me as Paul and we chatted for a minute or two while he waited for you, Mr. Diplomat."

"And what did you chat about?" Brummell inquired.

"Oh, this and that. Train travel in the winter. The waters of the Mediterranean compared to those of the North Atlantic."

"So, you spoke to him about your recent trip?"

"Well, only obliquely. He asked where I had been recently, and I mentioned I had spent some time abroad. That was what got us onto sea travel, and then to trains, I suppose."

Brummell pressed forward. "Any impressions of him? Did he talk at all about his reason for travel, or his work?"

"Let me think," she said as pointed her holder upward and inhaled deeply. Her exhale came a moment later, accompanying her words, "Not really. He said he traveled pretty extensively for business. His questions about my travel were…rather unmemorable. He struck me as harmless, if a little milquetoast."

"So, dull," Robinson offered.

"Yes, dull. Forgettable." She glanced upward, as though stumbling upon a thought. "Really, I'm surprised I remembered his name." Returning her gaze to Brummell, she continued, "Probably because he threw me over so rapidly for you. You enter the lounge, and immediately he's by your side! Not that I minded, though. I'm not fond of train conversations."

"So why sit in the lounge so often?" Brummell asked.

"I'm even less fond of confined spaces like that of my compartment."

"So you don't like your compartment?" Robinson offered.

"Oh, it's fine. But I'd need a drawing room, at the least, to feel like the walls weren't closing in on me. And those are very expensive."

"You, perhaps…didn't sleep well last night as a result? It must be difficult for you, especially with the train stopped for an indeterminate period of time…"

"Yes, I never—" she caught herself and stopped short. "Ah, I see. Did I, in my insomnia, perhaps stroll back to the lounge after retiring? No, I certainly did not."

Robinson nodded sagely. "But, while awake last night, did you perhaps hear anything? Perhaps see something when you walked to the ladies' facilities?"

Her eyebrows shot up at this last suggestion. "Well, Mr. Detective, I can assure you that my business in the facilities is entirely my own. And, anyway, I didn't leave my room after I turned in last night."

"And noises—perhaps you heard something in the dead of the night. Or felt a chill?" Robinson prodded.

"A chill? I think not. I don't have a sixth sense about murders taking place near me, Mr. Robinson. But, noises? Well…yes. There was something odd late last night. Probably around 1:00 or 1:30. There was a tap—or a knock—very softly. And then another. And then, what sounded like a click—maybe a latch being undone." She lowered her holder and shrugged, "I'm not sure."

The two men exchanged glances and Robinson continued, "At 1:00 or 1:30, you say. Two soft taps or knocks, and a click."

He duly noted this in his little book. "Was this at your door, outside it..." he trailed off, hoping to allow her to lead.

"Not at my door. Maybe next door. Or down the hall. I'm not sure. I didn't think anything of it at the time."

"So, next door...that would be Miranda's room, yes?" Brummell asked.

"Yes, we're next door to one another. But, like I said, I'm not sure it was *from* next door. Sound carries strangely on trains."

"Yet you remembered the noise," Robinson said rather than asked. "Just as you remembered Paul despite his own...forget-ability."

Her cheeks flushed as she shot back, "I don't like your implication. You asked me questions; I answered them to the best of my ability."

"Now, now, Mrs. Cohen, I implied nothing," he responded. "In fact, I found that Mr. Schmitt indeed possessed a unique property: simultaneous inconspicuousness and, well, for lack of a better word, *flash*." At her arched eyebrow, he elaborated, "He was both as bland as white bread and as noticeable as a fox amidst a flock of chickens."

Brummell said softly, almost to himself, "He wore a fashionably-cut suit, but it was made of inferior material and clearly worn rough. The opposite of what you would expect."

"Something to add, James?" Robinson inquired.

"Just thinking along with you. Mr. Schmitt indeed seemed to...face in two directions, as it were. Maybe that's why we all recall him clearly despite our first judgments of him."

"Perhaps," said Robinson.

"How did you know him?" the woman interjected. "I mean, he was clearly waiting for you in the lounge tonight and you seemed like old friends." A hint of accusation had slipped into her tone.

Raising a hand to forestall further inquiry, Robinson interposed himself. "Mrs. Cohen, if I may, a final question for you. Following your very regrettable loss, may I ask as to your future plans? Do you have work that awaits you in St. Louis?"

"Not really. I have our home, and my parents are close. I imagine I'll hire out as a calligrapher here and there should I need money, but I'm fine in the short-term." She sat up slightly, "I suppose you're not asking out of concern for the poor widow." A last, long drag on her holder finished the cigarette.

"No, Mrs. Cohen, I'm afraid I'm not. You see, the weapon used in the commission of the murder was a letter opener—a fine, mother-of-pearl encrusted one. It has on its handle what appears to be a monogrammed 'M'. I don't suppose that you, a calligrapher, perhaps a letter writer yourself, might have travelled with such an implement…?"

Only a moment's hesitation preceded her response, "No, Mr. Robinson. I don't travel with letter openers, seeing as they are largely decorative. And I'm hardly a professional calligrapher—I merely practice it as a hobby. Besides, I'm sure that a third of the people on this train have an 'M' in their names."

With that, Robinson dismissed her. Her brisk, confident pace carried her the short distance back to her compartment, the eyes of both men surreptitiously following her for different reasons altogether than when she had entered.

CHAPTER TWELVE

Miranda Credo sat uneasily in the lounge, a slight slouch in her posture as she faced off with her examiners. Introductions had already been made, and Robinson was closely scrutinizing her tickets with a hint of a frown on his face. Brummell, looking unsteady and uncomfortable, was trying to comfort her with small talk. Robinson had pointedly *not* asked him to relate what he knew of Miranda before her arrival. All parties seemed to anticipate awkwardness in the conversation ahead.

The sun glinted off the snowpack outside, and all three winced. "Forgive me, Miss Credo," Robinson spoke, "but you were visiting friends in Norfolk?"

She cleared her throat slightly, beginning to reach for her small purse, but then thought better and sat up straight. "Yes, that's right, Mr. Robinson."

"Perhaps you could tell me about them?"

"What in particular?"

"How you know them? Their occupations?"

"Oh, well, they're a couple of girls I knew from school. They went east for war work a few years ago, but we kept up over the years. One of them is probably going to be engaged soon, so we did some hopeful planning." Her smile was warm.

"The war work they took, do they still perform it?" Robinson queried.

"No, they moved on after the peace. They both had secretarial pool experience, and were snapped up by shipping companies."

Robinson, setting the coach ticket from her connecting train to Washington down on the table in front of her, fixed her with a penetrating stare and countered, "It seems you chose a rather late train to connect to the *National Limited* for your return journey." Reading from the ticket, he noted the arrival of her northbound train into Washington at just 6:10, only minutes before boarding for her journey west. "Perhaps your friends kept you too long?"

"Yeah, I probably cut it a little close there!" she said with enthusiasm. "This is one of my many character flaws: a loathing of boredom and a passionate desire to avoid it at any cost. I do *so* hate to waste time waiting around at stations. It always feels like I have just enough time…to do nothing! So I usually, um, throw caution to the wind and show up just in time. Fashionably late, and all that." Brummell gave her a sympathetic smile.

Something in that smile worried her. Concern grew on Miranda's face, replacing simple confusion. "You said you were investigating an 'incident' onboard, Mr. Robinson," she noted, "what happened?"

"There's been a murder, Miranda," Brummell interjected. Her eyes went wide and she inhaled sharply.

"A murder! Who? *Why*?"

Robinson rushed to speak, shooting a side glance at Brummell for his presumption, "A Mr. Paul Schmitt, Miss Credo. You might remember him—a grey suit…he kept company with Mr. Brummell in this lounge before your arrival yesterday evening."

"Oh, him? He had a compartment next to mine. But, whatever for?" Her head jerked around to look directly at Brummell,

"Surely you don't think *James* did it!" Pivoting back to Robinson, she continued, "He was with me at dinner last night, and then we saw each other off to bed after a nightcap." The earnestness of her tone made Brummell blush.

"Well, to answer your questions, Miss Credo," Robinson began, "Mr. Schmitt was indeed murdered. Second, we are endeavoring to discover precisely why he was murdered, and by whom. Third, I won't comment on Mr. Brummell's guilt or innocence at the moment." At this, the younger man issued a snort of derision. Taking no notice, Robinson continued, "Finally, your timeline is not quite right, as Mr. Brummell and I both stepped off the train onto the platform at Keyser after you parted ways." He turned to look at his companion, "Isn't that right, James? And *then* off to bed?"

A measure of annoyance crept into Brummell's tone, "Yes, Mr. Robinson, that's about right."

"Oh," Miranda said, "I didn't realize. My compartment is here in the observation car, so I didn't see what happened after James went forward." She sounded genuinely abashed.

"That's fine, Miss, no trouble," Robinson mumbled, consulting his notes. "I believe, however, I also saw your face looking out from the corridor window at the Keyser stop?"

"Oh, yes. Of course. I felt the train stop, and just wanted to know where we were. My window looked out onto some railroad tracks, so I thought I'd look at the other side."

"And did you see anything interesting there?"

"Just people and snow, I suppose. More of the latter than the former."

Robinson licked his lips and changed topics. "Did you know Mr. Schmitt?"

"Um, no. Not really. We spoke once or twice—I definitely remember speaking to him last night when I came into the lounge. While he was sitting with James and before I took his place, I mean. But otherwise, no. I didn't know him."

Robinson paused before continuing, making a show of checking his notes. Brummell suspected it was all an act, but gave the older man right-of-way. "It has been suggested you were seen near his compartment a few times over the course of the journey," Robinson said, his tone ominously neutral. "And that you had a conversation with him shortly after boarding."

The woman arched an eyebrow, and began in a tone more somber than she had hitherto employed, "Well, Mr. Robinson, as a railroad detective I'm sure you're familiar with the layout of these cars—Mr. Schmitt was my next-door neighbor on this train, so it stands to reason I'd be seen around his compartment pretty frequently. And, yes, I do tend to pause here and there in train corridors." She kicked out one of her feet, displaying her red-heeled shoe and continued, "Try wearing these at sixty miles an hour and *not* leaning up against doors, walls, windows—whatever can be found, really—to keep from tipping over. I bet you've never done *that* in all your years travelling about." Both men laughed in spite of themselves.

"And did you happen to speak to your 'next-door neighbor' at any other time?" Robinson again probed.

"Well, perhaps…yes. At boarding, we spoke briefly about something entirely forgettable. Dining times, perhaps? I was waiting for my porter to stow my luggage, and I was right outside his compartment and he hadn't closed the door yet…" She trailed off, offering a little shrug. "Hardly a relationship of any significance, don't you think?"

Brummell resisted the urge to offer an 'of course not' in affirmation, and silence reigned for a moment before Robinson continued, "Forgive me, Miss Credo, but the walls between rooms are not very thick. Did you happen to hear anything last night from Mr. Schmitt's compartment?"

She blinked, considering her response. "I thought I heard… something. Just voices, really—muffled and low—from his compartment last night. I…I don't remember exactly when, since I was sleeping fitfully for a while before I really 'got down to it', as it were." Her reply was hesitant, her tone distant and indistinct.

"We made Keyser just before ten, so after then or thereabouts," Brummell offered. "Do you happen to remember if you got to sleep soundly before the train was stopped by the snow?"

Her hands stroked the leather of her purse as she considered. "I was asleep before we stopped. I didn't realize we weren't moving until I woke this morning."

"I understand you do some free-lance writing," Robinson probed in a different direction. At her acknowledgement, he continued, "As someone who is always writing—and with friends far from your home—you must compose quite a few letters. You know, to report to friends and acquaintances about all that you've seen and done. Gossip, information, that sort of thing."

"Oh yes," Credo answered, "I write letters pretty frequently. Not as much as I should, of course, but I do try!" Her voice was open and enthusiastic, clearly relieved to be out of the territory of dead men's voices and nighttime skullduggery.

"Do you happen to travel with a letter opener, Miss Credo?"

"A letter opener? No—I can't imagine being able to do that easily. I mean, it would cut through my purse or scratch other things…Who'd travel with a letter opener?"

"Of course, you're correct on that point," Robinson conceded. "But, you see, the murder weapon appears to be…a letter opener."

A stunned pause, followed by a wary "Oh" issued from the

young woman.

"And, Miranda," Brummell cut in, "the letter opener is monogrammed. With an 'M'."

A longer pause. "Oh..."

"Miss Credo," Robinson broke in, "this train is a small community. One of the passengers, alas, must be the murderer. It thus falls me to ask each of you in turn: do you have anything to say about your fellow passengers—or about the deceased—that might shed light on this case?"

"Well...not *really*."

"Please, Miranda," James asked, "anything, any detail might help."

"Well, the couple in the drawing room just up from me—the heavy-set man and his wife, both middle aged?"

Both men nodded, affirming that they understood.

"They seemed to be having," Miranda continued, "a 'cracking good row', as the Brits say, yesterday evening."

"Is that so?" Robinson asked. "Around what time?"

"Um. I had gotten back from the lounge before dinner, so half past seven or so? Maybe a little earlier."

"The husband was finishing dinner with Schmitt in the club car when I arrived around eight or so, so that fits," Brummell offered.

"And the cause of their argument?" Robinson asked.

"I don't like to say...but it seemed to have something to do with a loss. Or maybe something that was lost. They were distant enough from my compartment that I could only make out—accidentally overhear, I mean," she quickly corrected, "a word here or there. They were definitely shouting at each other, though."

"I see," Robinson acknowledged. He was still for a moment, and then flipped through is little notebook. Finally, just when

Brummell was about to prod him, he continued, "Yes, well, I think that's all I need to speak with you about for now. Mr. Brummell?"

"Um, yes. Miranda, I hope that you're…well."

"I'm fine, James," she interceded. "I'm not a fan of my good initial being dragged into all this, but," she cut herself off, exhaled, and smiled widely, "I'm sure that with you two on the case the innocent will go free and the guilty will perish!" Her forced enthusiasm, both men could admit to themselves, was strangely charming. "Or something!"

***

Miranda had gone, rejecting in the process Brummell's chivalrous offer to escort her back the handful of steps to her room, and silence held sway for a time.

"Alright," he heaved with a sigh, "let me have it."

"Let you have what?" Robinson asked.

"The lecture, followed by the questions."

Robinson arched an eyebrow and sat back in his chair, crossing his arms. "Explain."

"First, a lecture about letting my…well, my feelings for the girl get in the way."

Robinson nodded. "Consider it given. And second?"

"The questions. You didn't ask her a thing about me, about what we talked about." He paused for several beats. "About why our meeting in the lounge ended so rapidly. You didn't even keep her that long. So, you're about to ask me those things. You're about to ask me to put aside my baser instincts and instead use my powers of observation—honed as they've been in the cutthroat chanceries of Europe or so forth—to make sense of that young woman."

"Yep." The terseness and informality of the reply—*was that a trace of an Appalachian accent?*—would've rocked Brummell back on his heels had he been standing.

Casting chivalry aside, Brummell proceeded to recount his conversation with her at dinner down to the last detail. Robinson listened silently, nodding at moments but pointedly refraining from jotting in his little notebook as he had done throughout the other interviews. Finally, Brummell arrived at the end. Expecting further probing, he braced himself for the censorious words of the older man.

"And afterward, James? The lounge?"

"The lounge?"

"What happened in the lounge? I saw her arrive, hesitate at the threshold, and finally take the place of Schmitt at your side. I saw you speak, for a time. Then I left and you found me on the platform. James—what passed between you?"

Heaving a sigh, Brummell continued, "I don't know. She wasn't as engaged as she was at dinner. She seemed more distant, more standoffish. We talked a little about cities—Cincinnati, St. Louis, Chicago—how they compared to New York and Paris." He trailed off before resuming, "The spark wasn't there this time. It was a bad conversation about effectively nothing. Frankly… she seemed like a different woman. Less sure of herself, less secure, more defensive. Not unfriendly, really, but much more guarded than before."

"No politics this time? No discussion of your career? No talk about her work or aspirations?"

"None at all, on all three counts. We might as well have been strangers…which I suppose we are. Anyway, we sat like that for thirty minutes or so before she went off to bed. I walked with her, sort of—perhaps merely behind her—and said goodbye at her door. We said we might see one another at breakfast, but…I don't know; I don't think either of us meant it."

Brummell hung his head slightly, clearly embarrassed at having to recount the details of his connection to this woman and obviously abashed at his failure in the lounge. Robinson, a gentleman, averted his eyes as he pondered.

"Well, James," he finally spoke, "we have more work to do." Turning his head to gaze out the windows at the valley lit magnificently in the morning sun, he continued, "And buck up. You've done no wrong. And a woman's depths are never fully plumbed." Sensing that the younger man had lifted his gaze as well, he added, "Plenty of innings left to play. As they say."

***

Lucius winced when Robinson instructed him to collect the final interviewees but nonetheless marched down the corridor to the drawing room at the forward end of the carriage. The largest berth on the *Escort*, it had been occupied since Washington by the largest couple on the train, and the porter had already seen enough of them to know that what was to follow would be difficult. Though their position prevented the detectives from seeing what exactly was transpiring, fragments of a dispute drifted back through the corridor.

Finally, a pause and silence, followed by a woman's voice exclaiming "Murder!" And then the distant, overlapping voices resumed.

Lucius reappeared a moment later, alone and abashed, but confirmed that his charges would be along shortly. Robinson, who kept a small flask on his person for just such situations, privately regretted that Lucius's duties would disallow him from accepting the stiff drink he so clearly deserved. Dismissing the porter, Robinson said to Brummell, "Let's take this opportunity to have a look outside."

Together, the two men made their way forward to the vestibule. Looking first out the left-hand window, they saw only a drop-off that was moderate for several feet before gradually growing steeper. "This is indeed a hillside," Robinson noted.

"There's no way Tollo stepped down on this side," Brummell agreed.

Turning to the right-hand side, they opened the vestibule door and stepped down. The morning was icy, but placid and beautiful. Footprints had disturbed the snow all along the train. "The engineers and conductors," Robinson explained at Brummell's searching glance. "They have to walk the train when we've been stopped this long to make sure the carriages aren't obstructed."

"Well, let's look around anyway," Brummel responded.

And so they did. Staying to the footprints already made to save their pant legs, the two men milled about around the vestibule. Raising his head to look along the train, Robinson noted how the stately dark blue of the train cars seemed to be draped in the light cheerfulness of the pure snow. The black roofs were almost completely obscured. The train had paused not only on a hillside, but on a curve, and the line of coaches seemed to stretch around that curve into infinity. That hundreds of passengers were only now waking up to a scene so simultaneously disconcerting and magical—this confrontation of the steel and refinement and progress of modernity with the invincible force of Mother Nature—struck Robinson as poetic.

And then he remembered that his railroad had been delayed by that same Mother Nature, and the scene felt much less special. Perhaps that same delay had led to the disgraceful murder he now investigated. His fingers came to his mustache without conscious thought.

"Mr. Robinson," Brummell called out. When the other had turned around, he continued, "It occurs to me that, were I to try to hide something...sensitive...in a situation like this, I might try somewhere that was both obvious and convenient, but likely to be overlooked. After all, everyone will be searched rather intrusively when the police are able to reach us."

Robinson considered, and nodded. "Yes, James, that makes sense."

"And if I'm trapped on a train that is itself trapped, my options to hide things like, say, the illicit papers of a Soviet spy are rather limited."

"Right again."

"And so I'd likely spirit them away to a place close at hand, unobtrusive, and perhaps even likely to lead to their destruction—or at least the loss of the sensitive material."

"You think like a criminal, James. Is there something you want to tell me?"

"Only that we should probably look under the carriage."

Robinson nodded enthusiastically, and the two men squatted down, peering under the *Capitol Escort* and the *Loch Awe*. The roadbed—the raised mound of dirt and rock ballast upon which the steel rails sat—remained clean and relatively dry. The carriages had sheltered it from the falling snow, and the heat from the train had gradually melted most of the old snow overnight.

"Yes, James, come here," Robinson called out from his position underneath the rear wheels of the *Loch Awe*. The younger man responded, and together the two swept aside the remnants of snow from around an object placed directly in front of the carriage's wheels.

"A glass bottle, green," Brummell said, evaluating the object. "Broken already." He was right—the large bottle had been broken into at least two pieces, and a large portion of its body seemed to be missing. The torn label identified it as a bottle of Perrier water. "Decidedly not top secret documents," he added with clear regret.

"*Bon courage*," Robinson, staring intently ahead at the bottle in his hands, added with a flare of French that provoked a smile from Brummell. "It seems we've found the rest of our bar-side accident, James." Robinson, realizing he had neglected to mention the shards he found earlier, quickly filled in the younger man on the pieces of green glass he had found swept underneath the bar.

"Ah," Brummell responded at the end of the story, "that *is* an interesting connection. So…"

"How—and *why*—did it end up out here?" Robinson finished for him.

Retrieving the bottle with gloved hands, the two men turned to reenter the *Capitol Escort*. The shades in the window nearest the vestibule flickered as a body brushed up against it. "Come, James," Robinson said. "I think our final interview is about to begin."

***

Doctor Wallace Edmundson and his wife, Mrs. Emelie Edmundson—Robinson knew their names from Preston's manifest rather than introductions, which had not yet been made—were eager to ensure that all present knew the degree to which they found the entire situation rude, horrific, and disgusting in equal measure. Paused before Robinson's table, they had not let either investigator get a word in before their enumeration of the railroad's faults had begun. Clearly educated somewhere in the northeast, they both made sure to employ their prolific vocabularies as they detailed the inappropriateness of a murder on a train, the outrageous inconvenience of a train stopped by snow, and the intolerably shoddy quality of their drawing room's bulkheads, which they insisted let in too much noise. They were on the cusp of moving on to the perceived deficiencies of the train's cuisine when the woman suddenly paused.

"Aren't you going to write any of this down?" Emelie demanded, glancing down emphatically at Robinson's notebook.

"Mrs. Edmundson, I am a policeman, not a customer complaints clerk. There has been a murder on this train, as you clearly know, and we have important things to discuss. Now, will you and your husband please *sit down*?" Robinson said with a hint of exasperation creeping into the most authoritative tone Brummell had yet heard him use. His open hand beckoned them to the table.

Reluctantly, the two large figures maneuvered themselves into position. The fit on their side of the table was decidedly snug, and their mutual bulk intruded into one another's space. Brummell thought they looked like two circles overlapping and would have found it hard not to grin under different circumstances.

In this case, though, no one was in a laughing mood. The two had seated themselves and maintained an expectant silence, waiting for Robinson to make the next move. Robinson, happy to have control of the conversation delivered into his hands, waited, savoring the tension.

"May we begin with your names?" he finally asked. "To match them to our records from the manifest." He added, almost as an aside, his own name along with that of Brummell.

The man spoke for them both, "Dr. Wallace and Mrs. Emelie Edmundson."

The woman added hastily, her tone prim and correct, "Of New Haven and New York."

"I see," Robinson continued. "And from which of these

destinations do you travel today?"

"Well, neither," she responded plainly.

"You see, Mr. Robinson," Wallace cut in, "I'm currently employed in the west—New Mexico, actually—on government business. Since my work will last several years, we've rented out our homes in the north. Instead, we're travelling from Baltimore today."

"What sort of government work, Doctor?" Brummell asked. "What sort of field?"

"The field is physics," Wallace responded, a slight tick working its way into the corner of his right eye. "The work is," he continued as the tick intensified, "not very interesting to laymen such as yourselves."

"Oh, one never knows," Robinson countered. "Take Mr. Brummell, here. He also labors on behalf of the government. For the State Department. Perhaps he might be interested in your work."

"Then what is he doing investigating this supposed murder?" Emelie cut in.

"I'm a man of many talents," Brummell responded, not missing a beat.

"He's also a suspect that I can't spare the men to guard," Robinson added, glancing nonchalantly through his notebook. "Still, I'm sure he'd greatly enjoy comparing notes about your respective service to Uncle Sam." Steel had crept into his tone.

"Well, uh, Mr. Brummell," Wallace began, "I work on classified matters related to national defense. That's really all I can say."

"In New Mexico, you say? Well, I believe I catch your gist," Brummell conceded. Turning to his partner, he added, "Classified, indeed. Very much so."

"Wonderful," Robinson interrupted, shifting his attention to the woman. "Now that we've settled that, perhaps Mrs. Edmundson can explain what you two were up to in Baltimore."

"Our private business is entirely our own—and certainly no business of the railroad's!" she angrily parried. Turning to her husband, she continued her tirade, "I cannot believe these little men are allowed to talk to us like this! We're paying customers. In a drawing room, in fact!" Brummell wondered if her harrumphs had obviated the need for investigation by awakening the corpse behind them.

"Just tell them what they want to know, Emelie," a weary Wallace responded.

An icy stare fixed upon her husband before she finally spat, "We visited friends, and that's all!"

"So you know Baltimore well, then?" Robinson probed.

"We visit once a year or so," Wallace responded in lieu of his wife.

"And where did you stay on this journey?"

"The Lord Baltimore Hotel."

"Ah, yes, I know it. A fine hotel, very fine," Robinson replied. Leaning in slightly, he continued, "I imagine a sophisticated man of distinction such as yourself enjoys, say, horseracing?"

"Well, yes. Sometimes," Wallace said in a monotone voice.

"Have you taken in the Preakness in your visits to Baltimore?" Brummell asked, sensing Robinson's direction.

"Yes, I've been to the Preakness."

"And your wife?" Robinson asked. "Have you taken in the races, Mrs. Edmundson?"

"No. I most certainly have not."

"I see." Robinson paused to jot something in his notebook before continuing. "May I examine your tickets for journey from Baltimore to—I assume—St. Louis?"

"Yes, Mr. Robinson, we are travelling to St. Louis and then

further west," Wallace replied as he searched through his pockets for tickets. As he handed them over, he added, "We don't have our tickets from Baltimore. We just took a commuter local train this morning to Washington."

"A commuter local?" Brummell interjected. "Seems a rather rough way to begin a trans-continental journey."

"There's nothing wrong with saving a bit of money," Emelie replied, for once in a voice soft rather than shrill.

"Indeed not," Robinson stepped in as he returned their tickets. "Of course, it must have been odd for you, taking a local train from Camden Station when the *National Limited* itself would have been coming through that same spot later that day."

"No, we didn't use the B&O," Wallace replied. "We took a Pennsylvania local from their station, the one in midtown."

Robinson furrowed his brow, a gesture suggesting he had been wounded. "I see," he said. "Let's turn for a moment to our murder. Last night, in the area behind us, a Mr. Paul Schmitt was murdered by the thrusting of a sharp object into his chest." Emelie gasped audibly while her husband turned a shade paler. "Did either of you know Mr. Schmitt?"

"Of course not," Emelie said sternly.

"He occupied, in fact, the compartment next to yours. It has been suggested, Dr. Edmundson, that you actually shared a light dinner with Mr. Schmitt yesterday evening. In the club car."

"Oh. Yes. Well, he and I might have shared a table. What... er, what did he look like?"

"Grey suit. Dark hair. *Next door to you.*" Brummell provided, with emphasis.

"Right, right," Wallace said, looking down at the table. "Yes, we did dine together briefly. Random pairing. Crowded car and all that."

"And *madame* dined alone?" Robinson asked.

"Yes. In my room," Emelie explained evenly.

"Why, Mrs. Edmundson?" Robinson continued.

"I was very tired."

"It has been suggested that there was some sort of problem or dispute in our near your cabin shortly before dinner," Robinson parried. "I don't suppose you could help clear that up for us."

"Dispute? No, of course not. We were upset at the shoddy quality of our room, of course. Perhaps that's what you so obliquely refer to."

"There also seemed to be a dispute of some type in the club car, Dr. Edmundson," Brummell added. "With the attendant. After your little dinner with Mr. Schmitt."

Wallace cocked his chin up slightly and answered, "That crook was trying to overcharge me. That won't do for me, no sir."

Robinson paused slightly, offering no comment on his answer. "Moving on," he finally said, "How would you describe Mr. Schmitt?"

Wallace wrinkled his nose. "Plain. Common, really. Forgettable."

"And what did you talk about?" Brummell asked.

"Nothing. The news, I think." An awkward silence descended, the investigators staring hard at the fat man. A thin sheen of sweat had appeared on his forehead. Brummell shivered slightly at the car's dropping temperature.

"So he did not ask about your work? Or your past? Or your reason for traveling?" Robinson asked, a hint of concern on his face.

"No, of course not," Wallace said, continuing with a flash of anger, "Who said so?"

With his subject properly rattled, Robinson ignored his question and continued, "I imagine you both have many friends that you stay in touch with via the post. Have you written any letters on this particular journey, perhaps describing how you enjoyed Baltimore?"

"I handle the correspondence for this family," Emelie interjected firmly. "And no, I have written nothing to anyone about Baltimore. I mean, really, what would one say? Dreary place."

"You don't like to visit Baltimore, then?" Brummell jumped in.

She blinked twice before continuing, "Not at all. Baltimore is lovely. That's why we visit, after all." She managed a slight smile. "In January, however…"

"I see. So, you do not travel with a letter opener, Mrs. Edmundson?" Robinson came to the point.

"No, of course not. What use would I get out of such a thing? These compartments are already so small, we're forced to make due with only the barest luggage allowance. There's no room for anything as silly as a letter opener! And to think that we pay such premiums to utilize your service, Mr. Robinson! You and your railroad should be ashamed!"

Ignoring her censure, Robinson switched subjects. "Given that you did not dine—and, I assume, did not make use of the lounges beyond your short dinner, Dr. Edmundson—I imagine you have nothing of material importance to this case to add about your fellow passengers."

"I'm afraid not."

"Oh, wait," Robinson said, shaking his head in self-reproach. "I did hear something about you being in the lounge last night." Brummell's eyebrow shot up; he had not been made privy to this particular point.

"Oh, right. I was just looking for a newspaper, that's all."

"And did you succeed?"

"No, actually. I wanted an edition they didn't have." Anticipating his next question, Wallace continued, "I had already read the papers they carried."

"Oh, of course," Robinson stammered slightly. Only at this point did Brummell realize that he was playing a role for the difficult couple, and he wondered at the significance of Robinson's course of questioning. Robinson continued, "There has been a suggestion that a meeting occurred somewhere in your car last night. We thought you might have heard something, perhaps coming from the room of your neighbor, Mr. Schmitt."

"No, sorry," Wallace answered, "we must've been sound asleep."

"I thought your walls were quite poor at keeping out the noise," Brummell said sharply, finally anticipating one of Robinson's little tricks before he had sprung it. "I overheard you…expressing your concerns to the Pullman men at Keyser."

"Well, I suppose we were so exhausted from these hideous conditions that we finally fell asleep!" Emelie answered, equally sharp.

Robinson allowed an uncomfortable period of quiet before finally dismissing them. They struggled for a moment to extricate their bulk from, first, each other and, second, from the confined quarters of the table. Emelie, of course, left in a huff. Her husband was more restrained, looking both investigators in the eye before turning to follow his wife.

"Well done," Brummell said, addressing his companion. "On the issue of the meeting in Schmitt's room, I mean. Caught them square in a lie."

"Perhaps, but the question of why they lie matters even more to me. And upon *it* may rest this entire affair."

Lucius again appeared, requesting instructions. The suspects had all been interviewed, and the train was awake. Robinson expressed a desire to be alone, and asked Lucius to rouse the suspects and gather them in the dining car, under guard and sealed off from the rest of the train. Brummell he dismissed to his quarters, offering his thanks for his assistance and telling him to bring his insights to the group meeting.

"You don't want to hear them now?" Brummell asked, surprised and a little hurt.

"No, James," Robinson replied. "I am on the verge of reconstructing this case in a way that makes sense. But the truth is still hazy and indistinct for me. I need to be alone for a few minutes—to feel my way through the lies and distortions that besiege this affair."

As the younger man stood to go, Robinson called after him. "And, James. You, too, will have to be under guard as we enter these final moments."

The other said nothing, but turned and offered a brave nod before exiting.

CHAPTER THIRTEEN

Lucius and Brummell had gone forward according to his instructions, and Robinson was alone in the observation car. Alone, that is, except for the corpse. Except for Mr. Schmitt.

The sun was up, and the snow glistened beneath skies of Titian blue. The coffee in his cup had long gone cold, but he cradled it anyway. The motion felt normal, and normality was a thing to be cherished amidst an affair that so deeply confounded his reason—the reason of a man whose mind worked with the same unforgiving, calculating efficiency as the railroad for which he labored. He sipped it slowly. Robinson liked cold coffee, the way that the flavors played differently on the tongue than when it was hot. He also liked hot coffee; it was only lukewarm coffee he despised. It couldn't make up its mind, trying to be everything at once. It was uncertain and indecisive and noncommittal.

He shook his head softly. This investigation was a *lukewarm* affair.

Sitting down the cup with his right hand, a swift movement of his left produced his pocket watch. Its stately dial proclaimed the time to be ten after eight. A whistle howled at the front of the train; Robinson knew it meant that the snow-clearing crew from Grafton had broken through. It would not be long now.

Closing his brown-gloved hand around it, Robinson's fingers eclipsed the dial in an effort to ward off his frustration. *No time*, he thought to himself, *no time at all.* Finding his hand insufficient to the task, he wearily shut his eyes as well. Time, circumstances, pressure—all were contributing to the cloudiness of his thinking. Everything about this case felt enveloped by a drapery of insulating velvet, an obscuring, blocking, suffocating cloak defying his attempts to order the events and objects and personalities populating this peculiar little drama. So many seeming to lie, so many seeming to possess a motive to kill, all seemingly ignorant—or were they merely feigning?—of the real significance of the death of Paul Schmitt.

That man, Robinson thought to himself. *The one who orchestrated this trip. Who lied and manipulated for purposes yet unclear. That man, the spider at the center of the web. Dead, perhaps caught in his own web…but aren't we all, at this point?* Stroking his little trapezoidal mustache, he considered the analogy of the web. It traps, ensnaring whatever comes close to it. *And yet…there is at least one item that seems to have escaped the web: the information he must have certainly have carried. The information that* had *to have been in the mysteriously unlocked documents case. The information matching the code key he so carefully concealed yet kept so conveniently close.*

Tired of the charade, the railroad detective turned about suddenly and angrily ripped down the flimsy barrier of sheets that had been hastily erected to conceal the body. A burst of cold air greeted him, as the windows he had ordered cracked to forestall decomposition had filled the chamber with the icy breath of winter. "The web that you spun, Mr. Schmitt," he said softly, despite the frustrated rage he felt bubbling up from within, "what did it trap? What did it allow to escape? Why *here*? We are on a train—a sealed community with finite space and finite opportunities for murder…and for theft." He paused for a long time, thinking with furrowed brow. "Desperation. Desperation attends this crime. And the desperate creature is far more likely to succumb to the trap of the web. What did the web that you spun here entrap, Paul Schmitt…that it now conceals?"

And then it happened. Finally inspired by anger and frustration, he had noticed something new. The corpse's left foot, clad in a nondescript black shoe, seemed slightly at variance with the right. Crouching down, Robinson realized what it was: the left foot rested ever so slightly off the floor of the coach. Lifting it slightly with his hand, he discovered a book of matches beneath.

He stared at it for several moments before reaching to retrieve it, knowing already what he expected to find there. Discovering his suspicions were correct, he replaced the book where he found it, rose, and looked with clear eyes at the scene. It made less sense than before, but perhaps that was a good thing. Like the snow clearers ahead of the train, he had to apprehend all the detritus in his path before he could effectively sweep the lot of it aside.

He was tired and rubbed his eyes, but the motion only reminded him of the ache in his shoulders. Tension, he knew, gripped every inch of his body as much as it did his muddled, tired thoughts. He shivered against the cold now unleashed from the lounge. His eyes turned futilely in the empty car to the empty bar. He wished he had a drink, a fine Scotch, to untangle his muscles as much as his mind. To warm him and light anew the pilot light in his brain that had seen him through so many cases over the years.

And, in that moment, it began to come together for him.

Each suspect's face flashed before his mind's eye. The professor. The widow. The young man. Stock characters given life in his interviews by their foibles and fears and speculations.

Which found itself here last night? What did it feel as it plunged the weapon into his chest? What did it think when it stepped back from the scene and…and, *what*?

"And when this character *then* went to work," he said aloud decisively. His eyes shot to the ashtray beside the corpse, and then to the chaos of his blood-stained chest. And then, in his mind's eye, to the case of documents in Schmitt's compartment. And somehow, in the midst of these glances and gazes and thoughts, he finally began to think like the killer.

To think like an animal seized in a trap—persecuted, desperate, and out of time—is not easy for a man of Robinson's years and success. But think he does, tracing within the narrow horizons of the crime scene a possibility…a *path of escape* for the murderer. Imperfect and hasty, but clever and bold.

And so Robinson rushes for the exit to find a porter.

CHAPTER FOURTEEN

Outside, the scene was placid as a whistle suddenly pierced the glacial air. The crews from Grafton had finally broken through the small avalanche that had delayed the train, and the engines thundered their preparedness to resume the journey. The sun was bright and the sky was clear and the snow was blindingly white and pure, interrupted only by the browns and dark greens of the trees that had withstood the frigid ache of the storm and the velvet uncertainty of the night.

Inside, the scene was tense as the *National Limited*'s passengers awoke. Lunch would be delayed, the passengers were told, just like their train. The dining car had been cordoned off, as had the cars at the back of the train. Though the staff were tight-lipped, rumors flew up and down the aisles from the club car to the sleepers. Three men were dead, stabbed through the heart. One woman had thrown herself in front of the engines in a fit of despair. A long-lost Romanov princess had been discovered riding in a second-class sleeper. So went the *vox populi*.

They did not know that it was the denizens of the first-class rooms on the *Loch Awe* and the *Capitol Escort* that assembled in that dining car, brought there under escort by a force of porters and conductors assembled to compel their attendance and guarantee their safety. Seven strangers, unknown to one another save for the accident of travel, sat together at four tables laid with demitasses of coffee and glasses of spring water and attractive little flowers in bud vases. The dining car manager had insisted that his guests be well served, even in the midst of a murder investigation. The guards stood off awkwardly a few tables away, uneasy at the prospect of a wolf concealed amongst the sheep.

Into this scene walked, finally, Ellicott Robinson. His fifty-odd years had sapped little of the spry energy that had characterized him in his younger days, but around him still hung a weariness—a sense of burden that decades of service and, particularly, the late war had draped around him. Dressed in his fine green tweeds, with his rich silk tie fixed to his neck and his little trapezoid of a mustache immaculately configured, he seemed every bit the commanding gentleman that his role now required him to be. He cleared his throat and began.

"Ladies and gentlemen, I have asked you all here to reveal the results of my investigation into the death of the man calling himself"—eyebrows arched on several faces at his phrasing—"Mr. Paul Schmitt. The road is now clear, and we will shortly be with the police in Grafton, to whom I will present my conclusions," he pivoted his head, examining each face in turn. "I will begin with the facts as they were known to me at, or very shortly after, the moment I found his body in the observation car."

Clasping his hands behind his back, he began to pace slowly forward. "I first took notice of Mr. Schmitt conversing in the lounge of the observation car with Mr. Brummell—a young man whose acquaintance I briefly made in the club car earlier that night—at around nine o'clock yesterday evening. This jogged my memory," he said as an aside, "and I recalled seeing these two figures in conversation earlier, in the club car in the front of the train."

Resuming his main narrative, Robinson continued, "That evening, I also noticed him speak to the ladies I later discovered to be Miss Credo and Mrs. Cohen. He stepped out onto the platform at Keyser, but he seemed to retire to his bed afterward. I, too, retired not long after to my section, where I worked until I felt the train stop suddenly. That was at 12:10 in the morning, precisely. I later discovered that the train has encountered a small avalanche, and must stop until it is cleared."

Pivoting on his heel as he reached the end of the room, he paced back down the aisle the way he came. "Sometime after that, I am disturbed by movement outside my door—I later discover this to have been Lucius tending to the urgent questions of Commander Tollo regarding the train's lack of progress. It is not until 2:13 that I am impelled to leave my section and investigate—not the absence of locomotion—but rather a noise…a…pounding or a *stomping* coming from the direction of the rear vestibule of my car. Rising, I find no one present and no signs of activity. Save, of course, a slight chill as I pass through the vestibule and a small bit of moisture on the metal walkway between cars. Later investigations suggest that I encountered the remnants of a short sojourn taken by Commander Tollo outside the train." He paused, allowing the passengers time to surreptitiously steal accusatory glances at the handsome young officer.

Looking finally to Tollo for confirmation, the officer nodded, "That's right. I wanted to see what was going on outside." Flashing the room with his best grin, he added, "It was a bit too cold—and I prefer my water in its liquid form." Miranda laughed unsteadily at that, while Croyden merely scowled.

Robinson resumed his narrative, "Finding nothing, I walked

further back, thinking the sound might have come from the observation car. Entering, I find a man. Stabbed to death."

Arriving back to his starting point, he spun again to face the crowd and removed from his bulging jacket pocket an object wrapped in a towel. Unfolding it to reveal the letter opener, he continued, "Stabbed, that is, with this." Holding it up while keeping the towel's surface between him and the object, he allowed the passengers to gaze. "A fine object inlaid with mother-of-pearl…and monogrammed in black enamel."

"That's an 'M'!" Doctor Wallace Edmundson declared.

"No, it's an 'E'," countered Mrs. Mary Cohen.

"No, no: a 'W'!" Professor Robert Edward Croyden interjected decisively

"Yes, it is indeed ambiguous," Robinson cut in, forestalling further comment. "So stylized, so angular, so *deco*," he said with an accent on the final word. "Suggestive, certainly. But exactly of what…well, that is less certain. We shall set it aside for now." He suited action to words.

"What did I know about the dead man at the time? Virtually nothing. I had seen him, to be sure, on the train. I had also seen him in conversation with various other passengers—but, of course, none of this is abnormal in any way. Except, however, the fact that I had seen him twice—*twice*—in discussions, at different times and on different parts of the train, with the young man I had met earlier that evening. This young man, Mr. Brummell, is a diplomat returning from Europe, just off the *Queen Mary*, in fact. So, why did these men—ostensible strangers—spend so much time in one another's company?"

He paused, raising a hand to wave off the topic, "We shall see momentarily. I just said that the letter opener's monogramming was suggestive. Well, there were other suggestive items as well, as a search of Mr. Schmitt's person revealed."

Reaching into another pocket, his gloved hand withdrew the silver watch chain. "First, this. A silver watch chain, found clutched in Mr. Schmitt's closed fist. A watch chain I recognized as belonging to Mr. Brummell." He laid it upon a table and reached again into his pocket. "Second, this. A match book, opened." He flipped its lid closed as he spoke, revealing an artwork of the *Queen Mary*. "When closed, it advertises the Cunard Line's *RMS Queen Mary*." Addressing the crowd and looking pointedly away from Brummell, he added, "And I note the presence of a cigarette, barely used, in the ashtray by the corpse. With it were the remnants of a matchstick likely from this book."

Tossing the matchbook onto the table in disgust, he turned suddenly on Brummell. "Mr. Brummell, enlighten us if you will as to your full name."

"James Matthew Brummell," he responded evenly.

"James *Matthew* Brummell," Robinson repeated back to him. Spinning once more to address the group, he continued, "We have only your word that you do not go by your middle name in common conversation. Thus, all the evidence I have given you points to young Brummell here as the probable murderer. The watch-chain, which so many of us noticed him using—"

"Wait," Brummell interjected, "you questioned people about me when I wasn't around?" he sounded more hurt than indignant.

Shrugging in response, Robinson resumed, "To continue: the watch-chain, the book of matches from the *Queen Mary*, and a letter opener with the suggestive monogram. All point to James. But, most of all, the fact that Mr. Brummell—alone among the passengers I had observed—seemed to have a real connection to Mr. Schmitt. So, tell us: Why, Mr. Brummell, does such a connection seem so apparent?"

Clearing his throat, Brummell answered, "Well, because we

had met previously."

"Precisely," Robinson continued. "Upon questioning Mr. Brummell, I discovered that he and Mr. Schmitt had shared a dinner the previous evening on the *Constitution*—a train of the Pennsylvania Railroad"—Brummell was certain he detected a measure of jealous hurt in Robinson's voice—"while *en route* from New York to Washington. Finding that they both intended to travel the next evening on the *National Limited*, they agreed to meet in the lounge to continue their discussion."

Opening his hands to his audience, Robinson adopted a conclusive tone, "All of this evidence is sufficiently solid to lead to Mr. Brummell's detention, at the least, on the theory that the two men met in the lounge again after it had been deserted. They talked, they smoked, and they ultimately quarreled with the result that Mr. Brummell's watch chain was yanked off his person by Mr. Schmitt and that Mr. Schmitt ended up with a letter opener—monogrammed with an 'M' for Matthew, which for all we know is the name Mr. Brummell chooses to go by—stabbed through his heart." Several necks snapped around to observe Brummell's reaction. He maintained an outward passivity, but his silence was deafening.

Robinson allowed the accusation to linger in the air for a moment before continuing, "To this evidence, however, I must add a further complication: the book of matches from the *Queen Mary*."

"You already said that!" Professor Croyden exclaimed.

"No professor, my intention is additive: *another* book of Queen Mary matches, which I found during my final canvass of the scene shortly before I came here."

"So there were two matchbooks?" James asked.

"Precisely. The first, I found on his body. The second, beneath his foot. Two books, both of which seem to have come from you, James," Robinson answered.

"But we know where the first book came from—Schmitt must have taken it on the *Constitution* after our dinner. I distinctly remember giving him a light from that matchbook, and he must have taken it when I put it aside. Thus, it was on him when he was killed."

"Yes, this is indeed the explanation you gave me under examination. But the second?" Robinson prompted.

"I...I have no idea," Brummell responded with exasperation. "I suppose I might have had another one," he said as his hand subconsciously went to his waistcoat pocket, "I always carry several that I pick up when travelling. But I don't remember specifically."

"This is absurd!" Miranda Credo shouted. "You're suggesting James randomly murdered someone he had met only the day before over...over what, exactly?" This exhaled loudly through her nose. "This makes no sense!"

"Perhaps, Miss Credo," Robinson answered, "but as a reconstruction of events based on the evidence we have available, it is reasonable enough to assure that Mr. Brummell will be taken by the local police to be the chief suspect and detained."

"But what motive does he have?" Mary Cohen asked evenly. "Are you suggesting he's a madman?"

"Mrs. Cohen asks for a motive, and I can supply it." Reaching into his breast pocket, he withdrew Schmitt passport and held it up for all to see. "This is Mr. Schmitt's passport—unused, by all appearances. Yet, within it are concealed papers identifying Mr. Schmitt...as an agent of the Soviet government!"

Gasps echoed throughout the carriage. The porters and conductors straightened up at the invocation of the foreign threat. "Yes, a Soviet spy in our midst. A man dedicated to the rooting out of secrets and the corruption of those who hold them."

He glanced down and to the side at Brummell, "And thus the last piece of the puzzle falls into place. The young diplomat confronted by the spymaster. Perhaps he has corrupted him, perhaps he merely intends to. But something goes wrong. Rage and passion—perhaps simple patriotism—enter into the equation, and the spy is killed by the diplomat."

"That didn't happen," Brummell said evenly. "But I bet the Grafton, West Virginia police would believe it did."

"Fortunately, James," Robinson continued, "you're dealing not with the local police but with the finest railroad detective there is. And I know better than to mistake the story as I just told it to you for the truth. To begin with, this train has no shortage of possible motives for the murder of Mr. Schmitt, nor of candidates for the spilling of government secrets." Looking from face to face, he began to enumerate, "First, an officer of naval intelligence stationed at Norfolk. What information might you hold about the movements of our fleets?" Robinson smiled slightly before continuing, "How many years have been in the service, Commander *Mario* Tollo?"

"Eight," Tollo responded.

"And you were in submarines during the war?"

"As I said."

"Forgive me for saying so, Commander, but you look awfully young for someone of your rank and experience."

He only shrugged in reply.

Robinson nodded. "Tell me, did Mr. Schmitt perhaps approach you at any point during the journey? Perhaps to discuss your job and how…interesting it must be?" Robinson advanced slightly on the younger man, "Perhaps offering you a drink—an illicit drink, to be had later, late in the night in the middle of a dry state. In the middle of an empty car."

Tollo leaned forward, placing his hands on his knees. "I don't like what you're implying."

"And, maybe, just maybe, after that little meeting went askew you decided to silence Mr. Schmitt, perhaps in a fit of rage. Perhaps…just to be safe."

"No! That's crazy!"

"Is it, *Commander*? Then why do you lie to me about your little trip outside?"

"I'm not lying!"

"Ah, but you see, I know that you are." Turning suddenly to Brummell, he asked, "James, in our interview with this man, do you recall me asking him about the scene outside?"

"Yes," Brummell answered. "You said that the diesels facing off against that wall of snow and rock must have been an impressive sight."

"And you seconded this opinion, did you not, Commander?"

"Yeah, I did! What of it?"

"Then you lie! You see, ladies and gentlemen, though this train is advertised as an all-diesel affair, there is still a steam locomotive added at Keyser to help the train over the mountain grades. It is removed at Grafton, before first light, so that the passengers remain unaware." Turning sharply back toward Tollo he added, "A fact *you* would well have discovered if you had truly stepped outside to seriously survey the scene."

Tollo scowled in silence. Brummell interjected, "Ah, so that's what that lone steam engine was doing chugging up beside us as Keyser. And here I was thinking to myself, 'How could he have *seen* anything in the middle of the night?'."

"That's right, James, on both counts" Robinson confirmed. "And so our young officer here lied to me about his reasons for stepping outside that night: he saw no sights at the front of the train. I propose an alternative. We have all seen, *sir*, your fondness for drink; late at night, the train stops in the middle of a dry wilderness. This prompts your urgent questioning of the porter—you have entered into the early stages of alcohol withdrawal and are panicking." He licked his lips before continuing, "You simultaneously disturb my work, not that you would have cared had you known.

"When no satisfactory answer about the train's progress is returned to you, your hunger only grows worse. Finally, at about two in the morning, you rise from your compartment and make your way to the observation car. There, late at night, you hope to find the bar's supply of liquor unguarded. You stumble to the bar, finding the liquor securely locked away but knocking over in the process a bottle of Perrier water that shatters on the floor. You reach for the bottle as it falls, hoping to catch it, but you only succeed in fingering the neck with your bare hands. It slips away, falls, and shatters."

Turning away from the crowd, Robinson looked out the window and continued, "Worried the noise has given you away, you dart up and survey the situation. It is then that you notice Mr. Schmitt."

"I didn't murder him!" Tollo cut in, his voice panicked and angry. "He was like that when I came in!"

"Perhaps…but why should I believe a liar?" Robinson shot back, pivoting toward him. "Perhaps you killed him yourself. Perhaps you found him like that. But either way, in your moment of fear, you know you must eliminate any evidence of your presence. The shards of glass you sweep away out of sight with your feet, while you grab the largest remaining piece, roughly the top half of the bottle that you know must bear your fingerprints. Too afraid of the further noise that would result from destroying it under foot, you grasp it firmly, intending to dispose of it as you flee. You then *bolt*, forcing open the door to the vestibule.

"Ah, but alas, you find the snow and the dark and the hills unnavigable. There is no escape. Seeking to at least eliminate the incriminating bottle, you place it in front of the carriage's wheels, trusting in the train to get rid of the irrefutable evidence of your presence for you when it resumes forward. And so you return, stomping your feet to clear them of the snow you had encountered upon alighting, and slink back to your compartment."

Silence descended for several moments. Tollo finally spat, "Yes, I ran. And, yes, I didn't want anyone to know I had been there. But, no, I *didn't* kill him."

"Wait," Dr. Edmundson cut in, "you're saying a combat veteran turned tail and ran at the sight of a corpse? And that he was so afraid we'd find out he was there that he went to these absurd extremes with the bottle? I mean, if he was going to run, wouldn't we know to suspect him anyway?"

"No, Doctor," Robinson replied. "I am not saying a combat veteran ran. Because the man you see before you is not a combat veteran at all. He is a liar and a cheat and, if I am not mistaken, a deserter on the run. A man travelling under a false name, but unable to conceal his true fingerprints."

"What do you know, old man?" Tollo's voice cracked as he spoke.

"You deny this? You, the supposed submariner who calls a submarine a *ship* rather than the correct term, a *boat*? You, whose age and manner are in no way appropriate for the rank you claim to hold? You, whose base drunkenness is more suited to a boy than a man?" Robinson snorted derisively. "It only makes sense, of course, that you would run, young man. After all, you are not stupid, merely dissolute."

Turning his face to the group, he continued, "He knew the moment that body was discovered that everyone on this train would be questioned, everyone's backgrounds explored...and that he would eventually be found out—guilty or innocent of the crime—and returned to the naval base from which he had fled only yesterday, a simple seaman impersonating an officer. He knew he could not be here when that happened, and that he could leave no trace of his real identity behind to clue in the authorities to his involvement and put them on his trail. Hence, his failed attempt to run and his desperate need to eliminate surreptitiously his fingerprints from the bottle."

Fixing him with a hard stare, Robinson continued, "I stopped in to your compartment on my way here, boy. I noticed you had done a very thorough job cleaning it. I doubt I would've been able to pull a single complete fingerprint from the usual spots. Very thorough job, though I think your hoped-for opportunity to abscond will not present itself."

Tollo turned his face to the ground and muttered a curse.

"Look on the bright side," Robinson finished, "I imagine your *real* name has neither an 'M' nor an 'E' to contend with, which at least disconnects you from the murder weapon."

Tollo looked up, a single tear drying on his cheek. The recruiting poster officer was gone, and in his place stood a scared boy. "Yeah, you're right about that."

"Moving on," Robinson said, gathering his breath, "he is not the only person with potential motive to kill...nor to lie. Mrs. Cohen, you claim your late husband was a government agent, one privy no doubt to many American state secrets. Tell me, did you happen to come across any of those in the weeks it took you to bury him and to 'settle his affairs'?" She remained silent, staring sharply at Robinson. "Perhaps Mr. Schmitt offered you the opportunity to profit from this knowledge?"

"I will not dignify your wild speculations with a response," she answered. "To do so would dishonor my husband's sacrifice—

to say nothing of impugning my own character." Clipped and precise, her demeanor suggested disgust with the mere notion of her involvement.

"And yet, you lie to me and mislead this investigation!" Turning directly to her, he added, "Mrs. Cohen, where did you and your husband meet? The precise meeting, if you please."

She blinked, caught off guard by the question. "We met in college. Several girls from my school were invited to one his fraternity's dances." She looked up, genuinely quizzical, "What does that have to do with anything?"

"Because it occurred to me," Robinson replied, "that our makeshift dagger and the perilous question of its ambiguous monogram might have led us quite astray." He picked up the letter opener from the table and displayed it again to the crowd. "An 'E'," he said, indicating with his finger, "or an 'M'? Or even a 'W'?" He turned the implement to demonstrate.

"You know, so many people when questioned about this item responded with some variation of 'why travel with a letter opener?'. And, to be honest, I came to agree with them. Who would travel with a letter opener? Who would have need?"

Miranda suddenly sat upright, "Wait, you're a calligrapher!"

Robinson nodded sagely, "That's right, Miss Credo. Mrs. Cohen is indeed a calligrapher."

"So what?" Cohen interjected angrily, shooting Credo a dark look. "That doesn't mean I'd need to take a decorative letter opener with me everywhere I go!"

"And on that point, Mrs. Cohen, you are of course correct." Again, Robinson lifted the item for all to see. "But it is not on that point that you attempt to deceive me." Again, he rotated it to the 'E' and 'M' positions. "An 'E' or an 'M'?"

"I still see a 'W'!" Croyden countered.

"Neither," Robinson concluded. "Mrs. Cohen, once more,

where did you and your husband meet?"

"In college..." she trailed off.

"At a fraternity dance," Brummell jumped in, realization dawning in his voice.

Robinson concluded: "Thank you for confirming what I already suspected, Mrs. Cohen. This, ladies and gentlemen, is neither an 'E' nor an 'M', but rather a Sigma—a Greek letter used by collegiate fraternities and secret societies." Turning a final time to Mary, he added, "Secret societies like those from which our intelligence services so commonly recruit."

"I didn't kill that man," Cohen said hurriedly. "But...it *was* my husband's letter opener." She cocked her head to one side, averting her eyes. She began to aimlessly tap her foot, struggling against tears. "Just a stupid memento of his stupid little club. I hated it, but I didn't want to part with something he...*liked* so much. So I kept it with me, intending to throw it away—into the ocean, into a dumpster, off the train...but I never did." Tears began to run down her cheeks, and she looked up imploringly at Robinson. "That stupid little club got him involved with another stupid little club that ultimately got him killed." She breathed rapidly and deeply. "And now it might get me killed too." Defiant, she suddenly stood up, "But I didn't do it! It must have been stolen—I didn't even realize it was gone until you told me a letter opener was the murder weapon this morning!"

"Please, Mrs. Cohen, sit down," Robinson said, coaxing her to calm herself.

"So she's the murderer, fine!" Croyden interrupted. "Let's get on with it."

Robinson fixed the professor with a hard stare. Cohen momentarily forgotten, he turned his attention to Croyden. "You, my dear professor, feel qualified to cast aspersions and throw stones? You, whose...*peculiar* morality makes you entirely susceptible to blackmail? You, whose career has ended in scandal? You, whose bravado and bluster lead you to tell anyone who will listen of your important connections in Washington?" Robinson savored every word, allowing the disdain and contempt on every word to caress his palette. Though loathe to admit it, he enjoyed putting figures like Croyden in their places.

"Miss Credo reports voices were heard late last night in Schmitt's compartment. Was one of those voices you, Professor? Is that what you and Schmitt talked about in the club car before dinner and then later that night—Italian beaches, debauchery… and maybe, just maybe, how your troubles would only get worse if you failed to enlighten him as to the latest thinking amongst your political friends? How unfortunate it would be if someone talked to the press about your…character." Robinson strode forward menacingly, "Is that why you killed him?"

"No!" Croyden exclaimed, his frosty, haughty exterior penetrated and his fearful self exposed. "I didn't kill him! And I didn't know he was a spy!" His breathing became erratic as he continued, "We just talked about…opportunities. He…he said how a lot of people might be interested in hearing about how politics in Washington really worked…he said…he said something about a book. That's why I gave him my business card—I didn't know he was with the Russians! And I never once went to his compartment!"

"Wait," Brummell cut in, "what business card? We didn't find anything like that on his body. Nor among his papers."

"No, James, we did not," Robinson confirmed. He sighed and prepared to change targets.

"Tell me, Dr. Edmundson, the scientist working on an unspecified—and highly classified—government project in the west," Robinson said, suddenly pivoting to the fat man and his wife, "did Mr. Schmitt make you a similar offer?"

"What? Of course not!" he answered.

"But did you not, Doctor, share an intimate dinner with Schmitt last night? And are you not yourselves," he said gesturing to his wife, "also potential subjects of blackmail?"

"No, firstly. Secondly, what are you talking about?" Though his tone was calm, the fat man's hand trembled slightly as he sat down his glass of water.

Robinson clenched his fists, clearly angry at the other's stonewalling. "I found it odd, Doctor, that you took a train from the Pennsylvania's station in Baltimore rather than the B&O's Camden Station. Odd, not only because of your strange choice of an inferior carrier," Brummell suppressed a snort as Robinson continued, "but also because you stayed at the Lord Baltimore Hotel, only moments from Camden Station and the faster, more direct route it offered to Washington. Why, I wonder, did you make this choice? Mrs. Edmundson indicated you wished to save money by travelling on a local train to Washington, but the cab fare uptown to the Pennsylvania's line certainly must have added to your expense. Why, I wonder, multiply your cost in time and money?

"James," Robinson said, turning suddenly to the younger man, "do you remember an incident on the platform when you boarded?"

"Oh, of course. Dr. Edmundson there plowed into me. Made quite a scene."

"Yes, and did you observe as I did the man in the shabby coat that approached?"

"A rough-looking character—I thought it was strange that he'd run up to help, to be honest."

"Something you perhaps could not see, James, was the extraordinarily contrived nature of the whole affair. Dr. Edmundson's stumbling into you was not accidental. He was simply trying to escape that man. Causing a scene with you and attracting several railroad personnel to assist seemed an efficacious method to escape the people that man represented—people in Baltimore to whom Dr. Edmundson owes money. Money," Robinson concluded, "he borrowed to support his gambling over a period of years. Tell me, how did your horse do at Baltimore last season, Doctor?"

"Poorly," he said, averting his eyes.

"And I heard you searching out a newspaper quite urgently, earlier. Something about the latest college football scores, yes?"

"Perhaps I enjoy athletics," he responded with a hint of steel in his voice. His fat hands grasped the arms of his chair tightly.

"No, Doctor, I don't think you're terribly interested in athletics," Robinson countered. "I think you're a degenerate gambler on the run. I think your bookmakers, your *Baltimore* bookmakers, have closed their books to you, and now you must finally pay up. No more horses, no more point spreads, no more—what? Boxers, dice, cards? No more second chances to recover your fortunes through games of chance, certainly.

"This is the *real* reason you took an inconvenient Pennsylvania Railroad commuter train to connect with the *National Limited* further down the line instead of just boarding at Baltimore's Camden Station—you knew they would be waiting on you there. You certainly didn't expect them to send an associate after you at Washington when you failed to appear on the platform at Baltimore." He jerked his head sharply toward the man. "You see, Dr. Edmundson, I think you're desperate. And desperate men do desperate things."

"But that doesn't make him a murderer!" Mrs. Edmundson insisted. "That man just asked Wallace about our debts—not about government secrets!"

"Quiet, Emelie!" Edmundson hissed *sotto voce.*

"And was it last night that a deal was preferred in his compartment to pay down those debts…a deal, perhaps, regretted and rectified later that night in the lounge, through murder?" Robinson watched Edmundson—both Edmundsons—struggle to get out words of denial. The man resorted to mouthing the word 'no' as his face reddened.

"Never mind," Robinson said in disgust as he returned his attention to the group. "I return at last to the point where I departed: the supposed guilt of Mr. Brummell. Even after the possible motives I have suggested, his guilt still seems to beckon us forward. And, thus, I ask: With so many other possible motives—with so many lies and deceptions and misdirections—how could so many facts become simultaneously stacked against James *unless he were guilty*? To put it differently, how could so many pieces of evidence have fallen into place *randomly* if young James is innocent? They couldn't have, of course…unless there was *reason* behind their placement. And so I begin for you a new line of thinking. If James is not the killer, then forces are in motion on this train to consciously paint him as such. Which means that there is more intrigue to wade through than even this relatively simple story of the spy killed by his potential source."

He turned to his fellow investigator and said with sympathy, "You see, James, you have been framed. And framed not only by the murderer in this heinous act, who wished suspicion to be cast on you in his place…but by the *victim* as well." A stunned silence met this last point. Dr. Edmundson's jaw actually dropped, and even the downcast Tollo seemed to perk up with interest.

"*Why would Schmitt, the victim, seek to frame his own murderer?*" Robinson continued. "I submit that Schmitt did not *intend* to frame his murderer, but rather to frame Mr. Brummell for a murder he *himself* intended to commit…and that the real murderer likewise hoped to cast blame for his—or her—act on our blameless young diplomat.

"Yes, I say plainly: Schmitt intended to murder last night! It is the only explanation, and to understand how this can be, we must return to the fact that Mr. Schmitt was a Soviet agent… and we must introduce a few additional pieces of evidence that will help us reconstruct what really happened. Two days ago, Mr. Brummell and Mr. Schmitt met by chance on a train from New York. They talk, and Schmitt discovers that his companion is a diplomat—a person of natural interest for a spy."

Robinson unfolded a tissue removed from his pocket, revealing Schmitt's dual tickets from that night. "Behold, ladies and gentlemen, the first piece of evidence that the man calling himself Paul Schmitt intended to frame James Brummell. We have here four tickets—two railroad, two Pullman—for the same train, on the same night. Two will carry the rider from New York to Philadelphia; the other two from Philadelphia to Washington."

"Why would anyone buy train tickets like that?" Miranda asked. "Why not just buy one journey?"

"Why not, indeed, Miss Credo?" said Robinson. "Why not especially when one carried, as did Mr. Schmitt, an additional two tickets, ultimately unused," he said, producing yet more paper, "for a trip to Pittsburgh via Philadelphia?"

"His plans changed?" offered Mrs. Edmundson.

"Indeed they did," Robinson confirmed. "They changed because Paul Schmitt thought a wonderful opportunity had fallen into his lap. You see, I suggest that he is not merely a spymaster, but a mobile one. He travels constantly—this he told many of you quite openly—but he met not *clients* in his destination cities but rather *contacts* on the trains along the way. Unobserved strangers, they are immune from suspicion and investigation. Compromised officials, Soviet underlings, mercenary snoops—anyone could serve him when there was no way to trace their connection. Information is exchanged on these trips, often nonverbally. He was on his way to Pittsburgh for one such purpose, but with a twist…he intended to liquidate one of his assets. He intended to murder."

"Why would he murder his own agent?" Croyden asked skeptically. "This makes no sense!"

"This person had outlived his usefulness," Robinson answered, "and Mr. Schmitt intended to collect his last bit of intelligence…and then kill him." He ran a finger across his mustache, pondering. "I suspect that a Soviet spymaster in the United States is often forced to rely on agents…how should I put it? That are less than loyal to Moscow? Compromised, desperate men and women? Free-lancers, confidence tricksters, and charlatans down on their luck? Any of these candidates would find their usefulness decreasing with each success…and the potential liability they posed to Schmitt increasing the more they learned about his operation."

"You seem to know an awful lot about spycraft," said a more subdued Croyden.

"Indeed. During the war, I…well, I did my part for internal security," Robinson offered cryptically. "Back to the point. Schmitt knew an opportunity when he saw one: a young diplomat being redeployed to a position of public prominence important to American diplomacy in Europe."

"You suggest that he attempted to convert this young man?" Croyden inquired.

"No, not at all. You see, James is honest when protests he is of very junior status. He has little intelligence to share that could not be acquired elsewhere. Instead, what he offers is an opportunity to *embarrass*. What if a bright young governmental official—one with a promising career and shortly to be in the public eye—were to be found mixed up in a murder?"

Robinson looked to Brummell for an answer, and he responded, "It would be a horrible embarrassment for the State Department. And a blow to our efforts to promote the Marshall Plan to voters. A propaganda victory for Moscow, undoubtedly."

"Precisely. So, Schmitt makes a sudden change to his plans. He leaves your table on the *Constitution* before Philadelphia, purchases an extension of his journey from the conductor, and sends a telegram to his accomplice. The situation has changed, he says, and now we must meet on the *National Limited*; indeed, it was the remnants of the receipt for this telegram that I found, soiled by his blood, in his pocket. He then arranges tickets for them both—able, even at the last minute, to obtain berths in the off-season—and meets that person on this train. He will collect that agent's final information drop, kill him, and plant evidence suggesting Mr. Brummell's culpability. While the police are distracted by the case against Brummell, he will slip away." Robinson breathed deeply before continuing.

"The watch chain he steals from your compartment while you were in the dining car eating dinner, James—after all, he was careful to avoid an engagement with you at that time, and knew your room would be empty. He likely broke in with the intention of finding something—anything, really—to incriminate you. The watch chain, he figures, might be left on the victim's body, as though ripped off of you in the midst of a struggle...or perhaps it might even be used as the murder weapon itself. And, even if that fails, there is the book of matches he surreptitiously removed from your table on the *Constitution*—a sure way to link you to the body, or at least the scene and time of the murder, and misdirect the police."

"That seems rather thin, don't you think?" Croyden

demanded.

"Not at all. Not when you consider, that is, that Schmitt cared little for the legal niceties of guilt or innocence—he cared only that, first, he got away and, second, that some damage was done to his enemies in the process of liquidating a weak link amongst his assets. If James was convicted of a crime he did not commit, then wonderful; if being mixed up in this mess merely destroyed the career of someone considered talented and useful by the State Department…well, that is still a victory for him. Especially since Schmitt's inconvenient agent winds up dead either way."

Turning to the wider crowd, he added, "So many of you were at pains to describe Schmitt to me, after all. You struggled to define him, settling on words such as 'bland', 'plain', 'forgettable'… most of you seemed to pick up on, perhaps subconsciously, Schmitt's greatest asset: his ability to be forgotten, to disappear from memory and from sight. This allows him to escape with only a moment's head start—to adopt a new name and continue his mission here in America.

"But even the understanding that I have just presented—that Schmitt framed Brummell for a crime he did not get the chance to actually commit—is muddled by the evidence. You see, there is the issue of the second matchbook. Why would Schmitt bother to duplicate a piece of evidence pointing to James? And where did he find the second book?"

"I've been thinking about that," Brummell offered. "I used a matchbook to light your pipe in the club car last night. I might have left it behind, and it might have been from the *Queen Mary*."

"Or at dinner," Miranda interjected. "You gave me a light then." She paused. "Did you put that book back in your pocket?"

Robinson waved away both suggestions. "You miss the point,

my friends. The *how* of the matter is less significant than the *why*: Why duplicate the evidence?"

"For that matter," Brummell added, "why would he have used one of my matches to light *his own* cigarette in the lounge—wouldn't that place *him*—?" He broke off, realization dawning in his eyes. "Because it wasn't Schmitt that left the second matchbook," James concluded. "It was the person who murdered Schmitt, trying to make it look like I had done it—that we had had a conversation, a friendly one, that turned south. And that person lit one of Schmitt's cigarettes with the purloined matches, snuffing it out immediately and leaving the matchstick prominently behind. All to make it look like I was there."

"Precisely," Robinson praised him. "But the killer didn't know that Schmitt had *already* appropriated one of your matchbooks with the intention of placing it on the body of his *own* victim. Again," Robinson said, almost abashed, "to incriminate you, James. Hence, the two identical matchbooks are found at the scene."

The room was silent as the crowd considered the weight of Robinson's words.

"Finally," he continued after a moment, drawing from his pockets another large piece of paper, "there is this."

"A tourist's guide to Washington?" Croyden harrumphed, "Well, no accounting for taste even among spies."

Ignoring him, Robinson continued, "It was Mr. Brummell who first put me on to an interesting point: why would Schmitt be carrying a railroad guide to Washington, D. C.? Simple irony, perhaps? No, I think not. So, I examined it and, lo and behold, found something very odd—something that should not have been there." He opened its pages and displayed the carbon paper with the code key.

"Gibberish?" Dr. Edmundson asked incredulously.

"I think not," Robinson parried. "Rather, it is a code key for deciphering basic encoded documents. I hypothesize his agents were instructed to encrypt their information drops to him to guard against prying eyes; this would allow him—as copies distributed to his agents would allow them—to rapidly code and decode as needed."

"How does this play into the intended victim framing me?" Brummell asked.

"Because, James, this key is missing its mate: the sensitive information that was delivered in code. We have found no such encoded information on Schmitt, nor in his compartment, nor among his papers. It has disappeared, and was not to be found in the extensive search I made of your compartment at the beginning of this investigation. *Someone* must have taken that incriminating data—someone who knew about it because he or she had delivered it, and knew it would incriminate the real murderer if found. He or she was likewise at pains to find the code key, but it was elusive. No matter—the real murderer was likely hoping all the while that we would never figure out that there *was* incriminating data to be found at all. If *he* couldn't find the key, knowing it existed, then *we*, not knowing, would never locate it.

"But we *did* find it. And we found the Soviet documentation as well. And we were suddenly made aware of a powerful motive for the *real* murderer: the theft back of incriminating documents, and the silencing of a threat. No longer are we left with Brummell's intimacy with Schmitt as the only possible motive."

"Are you sure?" Brummell said after a moment's thought, "Perhaps I *am* the agent, and I stole back the data I originally gave him. I was there. I suppose I could've found the information I had given him, and then hidden it effectively under your nose."

"Do you remember when you made use of the toilet before

we began our interviews?"

"Yeah..."

"I took that opportunity to search your compartment a second time. And then I searched the toilet when you were done. Oh, and I made a cursory check of your suit pockets as I was straightening your tie."

Brummell, wide-eyed, just stared back at him.

"Anyway," Robinson pushed forward, "Remember the absence of anything incriminating among Schmitt's papers; I imagine our murderer did away with him in the lounge and then proceeded to rifle through his things, retrieving whatever materials he had already turned over and searching for the last bit of information—the code key—that would have clued investigators in to the presence of espionage. But the code key could not be found, because Schmitt had taken the simple but ingenious step of pasting it inside the most ordinary of documents to found on a train: the railway guide to the capital."

"So the posited information you're talking about...it's still out there? Or, rather, in here?" asked Dr. Edmundson.

"Yes. And it, if found, would point to the identity of the murderer by virtue of the information it contains." Robinson paused, shifting topics. "But there is one final piece of evidence found on the body." He withdrew the tube of lipstick from his coat and placed it upon a cocktail table next to Cohen.

"Not quite my shade," she said evenly.

Robinson, cocked his head to the side and conceded, "I suppose not, but then men can never tell, can we?" He smiled, but received only a cold stare back.

Turning to face Miranda, he received her spirited reply: "What—do you think I killed this man I have never met, and then left a tube of my lipstick behind...as a sort of calling card?" she asked, incredulous. "Worse still, do you think I'm the kind of girl that carries around multiple tubes of lipstick at once?" Her eyes widened in a mixture of real and feigned indignation.

Robinson's booming voice cut in: "*Why was Paul Schmitt carrying a tube of lipstick?*" He posed the question to the group with a frightening intensity, almost a shout.

Brummell raised his hand slightly, indicating he wished to answer. "If we go by the logic of the *Queen Mary* matchbook and the silver watch chain, then Schmitt was going to somehow use it to point the finger at me. Which would probably make Schmitt's intended victim—and, thus, his murderer…a woman."

Heads whipped around in each direction to the three women in the room. Emelie looked as though she might burst into tears; Mary remained cold and impassive; Miranda seemed dumbfounded by the revelation.

Exhaling, Robinson spoke wearily, "This question tortured me throughout the interviews. What use would this be? If it was to be used, like the matches, to point to James as the killer, then *how*? Perhaps to be planted on him, to link him to the body? If the intended victim—and thus, our real murderer—were a woman, was this supposed to have implied that James murdered her and then took her lipstick? That doesn't fit. Could it have instead been planted on Schmitt's body by the murderer to merely implicate a woman?"

Robinson sighed, but began again with renewed energy, his evident self-doubt suddenly banished. "No, it makes no sense. It *made* no sense, that is, until I conducted a final search of James's compartment on my way here. I searched not for a tangible object, but rather for a mark. And…I found one. Or, rather, several, on the back of his pillowcase. And the hem of his nightshirt. And then I remembered an incident earlier this morning when I straightened young James's tie. Inside his collar, on a shirt he claimed to be unworn, almost unnoticeable, was a small mark of red.

"Each one was subtle, barely evident. Each found in places where James was unlikely to find them himself, but that the police would undoubtedly discover in the course of a serious investigation. Each was added last night at the same time that Schmitt entered James's compartment to steal evidence to plant on his victim. All of these marks, ladies and gentlemen: *lipstick marks*, of the type suggestive of a woman's company last night. Of the type, that is, that would beg explanation from authorities investigating...the brutal murder of a young, attractive woman on a train."

The heads that had pivoted all over the carriage now slowly turned to view a single target: Miranda Credo.

"Yes, Miss Credo. The woman who so visibly joined James for dinner. And then for a drink. The woman who seemed so entranced by him at one moment, but fled the next. A seeming innocent among a group of passengers deeply connected to statecraft. And secrets. And scandal."

"Look, I don't know what you're playing at here," Miranda countered. "I never went near James's compartment, and I had no idea who Paul Schmitt was until you told me about him." She shook her head firmly, "What you're describing is entirely circumstantial."

"Ah, but what circumstances!" Robinson declared. "You, Miss Credo, a confidence woman skilled in charm. Skilled in manipulation. Did he pay you for your services in...what, seduction? Or something more wholesome? Did you ply the officers of Norfolk for their information, as you believed Schmitt was instructing you to ply young James here for his?"

Her head shook slowly as she turned it to look at Brummell, mouthing all the while a silent 'no'.

"When did you first suspect that he intended to eliminate you?

Was it the sudden change of venue from Pittsburgh? You see, I noticed your ticket from Norfolk put you in rather late to catch the *National Limited.* Your fellow travelers connecting from there all chose the earlier train, but you picked the later. I was foolish to not realize the significance of that fact immediately: a quick glance at the railway guide confirmed my suspicion that the train you took was the scheduled connection with the Pennsylvania Railroad's *American*...to Pittsburgh. And most certainly *not* to St. Louis, your claimed destination."

Her head stopped its negative motion, and she sat back in her chair. "You haven't a shred of evidence," she declared plainly. Brummell's brow suddenly furrowed.

"Do I not?" Robinson countered. "The tickets and lipstick paint a powerful picture—certainly one sufficient to satisfy my investigative instincts. Of course, I suppose the information drop from the agent would indeed be necessary to assure your conviction," he conceded.

"This troubled me, after all, this missing piece, this Rosetta Stone to the identity of Schmitt's fellow player in the game of espionage. And then I started to think like the murderer—a person hard-pressed by circumstance. The train is stopped in the wilderness; escape is impossible until it reaches civilization. The murder has been committed, the incriminating documents retrieved—but then what? They cannot be hidden effectively in the quarters of either the murdered or the murderer, and it is too risky to head forward through the *Loch Awe* in search of a better hiding place. What is to be done?"

He paused, sighing, "But, then it occurred to me how nice a glass of whisky would taste after this shameful affair concludes—frustration will do that to a man, you see. But, of course, we are in a dry state. The liquor is sealed away from the moment we reach Harpers Ferry until we make the Ohio state line. Sealed away...

in a cabinet in the *Capitol Escort*." His words sunk in slowly; the crowd followed in rapt attention as Credo sat impassively still.

"Where better to hide an incriminating document than the one place that would have remained both padlocked *and* easily penetrable by a slender piece of intelligence slipped," he paused, making a motion with his hands akin to the insertion of a letter into a mail slot, "through the crack? And so I had the liquor cabinet opened, and out came…this," he said, producing from his interior pocket several folded sheets of paper. "Behold the reason for Mr. Schmitt's attendance on this train…and behold the reason for his ultimate death. On these papers are a series of seemingly random numbers and letters. Seemingly, that is, until compared with the key found taped inside Mr. Schmitt's charming B&O guide to Washington. I discovered this only a few minutes ago, and though I haven't had time to decode it myself…I feel confident that it will tell a tale that points squarely at the woman calling herself Miranda Credo."

She sat there, her face reddened to match her clothes. Her lips trembled, but on the cusp of a retort, or a curse, or a plea it was not clear. Brummell could not meet her eyes.

"Very well," Robinson said mournfully, "if you won't enlighten us, I'll continue with my speculations. You arrived at Washington on your scheduled train and rushed to catch the *National Limited*. You then boarded your car and—as observed by our ersatz commander—you quickly deposited your encoded drop with Schmitt. This, I imagine, was the usual limit of your interaction—a moment only, in the hustle and bustle of a train… perfectly innocent and untraceable, just two neighbors saying hello.

"But then, something changed. He says he must speak with you, and that you should wait until things have settled and then you would talk. It was probably in the suburbs of Washington that he told you of your next assignment: a young diplomat *on this very train* carrying important information about the European situation. He told you to arrange with the steward to have him seated next to you at the second call for dinner—just as he himself had paid off a steward the night before to make sure Brummell was seated at *his* table then." Robinson paused, offering a weary, ironic smile. "You should also appear in the lounge after dinner, he suggests, and work him further. Seduce him, if necessary?" Credo stared icily ahead. "Well, no matter. Either way, you are to report back to Schmitt in the stillness and darkness of the empty lounge once you knew what James knew.

"If you weren't suspicious before then, I'm sure you were at that point. This wasn't how things normally worked. Schmitt never got this close to matters—and he never sent you on a mission in which he himself might become entangled.

"You prepare for your engagement and go the lounge for a pre-dinner drink, hoping to get the lay of the land. You've had no time to prepare or research, and you're feeling nervous and exposed. You strike up a conversation with Mrs. Cohen, where you discover she is an amateur calligrapher. This information you store away for later, as you do with everyone you meet on your missions.

"You then repair to dinner with young James and rapidly discover that, whatever his more charming qualities, he is in possession of no data worth risking your position over. Surely, you think to yourself, Schmitt can see that. Suspicions multiply in your mind.

"Schmitt had next arranged it so that you would meet James shortly after dinner for a drink, though you were supposed to make it look unplanned. You didn't realize that it was supposed to look unplanned because Schmitt himself had an engagement with James at the moment. You enter the lounge, and see the two men talking. He *never* talked to your targets. That was strictly against the rules. Something feels wrong. You panic, and turn back toward the corridor—as I myself observed in my peripheral vision.

"You then arrive at a moment of decision. Perhaps you are being sold out, betrayed to the American government. It doesn't matter. The walls are closing in on you, and you resolve to bolt from the train at the next stop. Seeing Mrs. Cohen in the lounge, you realize her room is empty, and an idea occurs to you. You disappear back down the corridor, quickly enter her room, and begin to cast about for tools to use in your own defense in case things go poorly for you. A calligraphy nib, perhaps? Cold steel, yes? If shoved with appropriate gusto in the right point, say the neck, it could kill. But, lo and behold, you find something far more suited to murder: a letter opener, decorative but finely sharpened.

"You return quickly to the lounge, taking up your engagement with James. You end it early with the intention of escaping at Keyser, but your reconnaissance out the window reveals that Schmitt has beaten you to the platform, and stands watch outside. Indeed, he had probably alighted for the very purpose of making sure you stay on the train and keep your appointment with him. Your appointment with your own execution.

"This plan foiled, you know the next stop is Grafton, and you plan to simply try again there—but when the time comes, the train is stopped in a wilderness awash in snow. There is no escape. You again panic. You know you must keep your appointment after all.

"The meeting time arrives: half past one in the morning. Mrs. Cohen, you hear at roughly that time a series of soft knocks, and then a click. This was the signal for the meeting. You respond to your master's call, Miss Credo. You go to the lounge, away from the thin bulkheads of the sleeping berths. You sense that danger is near. You remove the weapon you had stolen from your neighbor…and you plunge it into his heart."

Her hands had tightened around the arms of her chair, but still she was silent.

"And the thing that amazes me about it," Robinson said striding slowly toward her and leaning in, "is that you were right. He *was* going to kill you. He was going to kill you from even before he changed the location of your meeting. Even before he set you on the trail of a boy who knew nothing. He sat there, last night, with a silver watch chain in his hand." He crouched down, meeting her gaze and raised a finger to point back over his shoulder. "*That* was the watch chain he was going to strangle you with. Your neck…it's just thin enough for it to work, isn't it, Miranda?"

"That BASTARD!" she shouted. Hot tears began to stream down her red cheeks. Nobody moved to help her, no one said a thing. Robinson slowly drew himself back up to his full height.

"The deed done," he continued, "you rifle first through his unbloodied pockets in search of the papers you had given him earlier or, at least, the code key that would make them intelligible to the authorities. Finding none there, your panic intensifies. You remove his watch—so large, so bold that you've always wondered about it—thinking *it* might contain the key, folded and tucked away beneath its dial. In your haste, you miss the lipstick, hiding deep in the well of his pocket.

"But you are concerned with more than protecting yourself. You also need a patsy, a hapless victim to take the blame for your act of…self-preservation. So you quickly plant the distinctive matchbook young James had used to light your cigarette at dinner—you were apparently so entrancing he failed to notice you pocketing it—under Schmitt's foot, as though it had fallen on the floor in the midst of the encounter, to implicate him. You hope, of course, that the fact they had been seen speaking with one another combined with the matches will be enough to make James the primary suspect. But, just to make it clear, you remove one of Schmitt's cigarettes just before, light it—throwing the matchstick in the ashtray—and then snuff it out almost immediately. Surely the local police will see it now!

"Then, you hurry back to Schmitt's compartment. You smash the watch, quite sensibly wrapping it in a wash cloth to mute the sound, thinking to retrieve the code key you suspect hidden inside, perhaps under the dial. But you find nothing: only an ordinary, if rather unusually large, watch. To hide your involvement, you stow it in his dopp kit and place it out of immediate sight.

"You then move to the attaché case of worthless prop documents he carries about. *Voila!* You find your drop—a few slender pages, typed in code, of evidence that would incriminate you if translated—and take it back.

"Ah, but here is you dilemma: where to hide it? You can't leave the train—your footprints would be obvious in the snow even if you had somewhere to go, which you don't. You can't go forward into the next car—many in the Pullman sections, myself included, were still up and would remember you. You can't simply throw it away in the *Escort*'s waste bins nor keep it on your person—a police search would surely follow, of the car and possibly of its passengers. You can't simply chuck it out the window—the train is stopped, and the crew and, if necessary, the police will undoubtedly inspect it from front to back before it resumes its journey.

"You return to the lounge, casting about desperately for a place to stow the documents, but in vain. But then you look behind the bar and see the liquor cabinet. Sealed since Maryland, it might escape a search, or at least the initial stages thereof. If you're lucky, you might even get a chance to retrieve them before you flee. So, with great effort, you slip the coded papers through the open joints in the cabinet, meticulously, one by one. I found them there," he paused and removed a last, small piece of paper from his jacket, "along with this. A business card, with Professor Croyden's name on it."

Realization slowly dawned on the professor's face. "Why… you were trying to frame me!" he exclaimed to Credo.

"A piece of insurance, sir," Robinson answered for her. "She must have removed it from Schmitt's body at the last minute as a backup plan: if found alongside the papers, the connection might well have been enough to cast *you* as the primary suspect and give her time to escape. Especially since the key necessary to rapidly decode the documents and, thus, to discover her own involvement was nowhere to be found."

Robinson paused, and assumed a thoughtful, hesitant tone. "She didn't need a perfect plan, ladies and gentlemen. *Time* was all she needed: a little time, a little confusion, a little freedom to slip away and utilize the skills of the long con she knew so well to adopt a new name. Maybe even a new face. To kill off Miranda Credo and to reemerge as someone else entirely."

"Ingenious," Croyden mumbled with a measure of respect. Clearly, he had found one passenger that was certifiably interesting.

"Indeed," Robinson agreed. "So, tell me Miss Credo, do I have it right? No use lying given that you will shortly be in the hands of federal agents who will certainly make sure to translate these papers in full before they ever think of releasing you."

She exhaled deeply through her nose and finally responded, "I felt that he had matchbooks in his pocket when I found the business card. I should've checked them before I planted James's book on him. That was sloppy." She sighed. "I just flat-out missed the lipstick. Schmitt was a slippery bastard. I should have checked everything, every inch of every pocket. But I was too exposed, and I didn't have the time. I suppose I messed up."

"On that point, you're correct," Robinson conceded. "If you had found and removed the duplicate matchbook and the lipstick, your deception would certainly have worked, at least long enough for you to get away. You had no reason to suspect we would stumble upon evidence of Schmitt's real career and, from that and from the anomalous tube of lipstick, begin to piece together a plausible alternative to the suggested murderous intent of young James *all before we even reached Grafton.* We were fortunate to see through both your deception and his before events got away from us."

Finally looking up to meet Robinson's gaze, she stated defiantly, "It was him or me. You said as much yourself." Her eyes betrayed no doubt, no remorse—only annoyed regret at the outcome.

"And I believe that was the case," Robinson concurred, his tone that of one professional speaking to another. "Though it is merely a theory that fits the facts. Entirely circumstantial, and not likely to carry much weight in court."

Credo laughed, a deep and throaty release. "I'll never see a court. I know enough that I can be useful to Uncle Sam."

"Or they'll simply shoot you," Croyden interjected. "Tend to do that to traitors."

"I'm not a traitor," Credo parried. "Merely a professional. I don't *believe* in anything enough to really betray it. And the feds will treat me as such. An asset. Just as I've been for a very long time."

"I have one question," Brummell said sharply.

Robinson nodded. He felt for the younger man, but regretted that he was giving in to his emotions. Lovelorn declarations were inappropriate at times like this, in his view. "All right, James, ask it," he said, granting permission.

Addressing himself to Credo, Brummell leaned forward, resting his hands upon his knees as though about to pounce. "The key to the attaché case—the one in Schmitt's cabin—what did you do with it?"

Robinson broke into an unabashed smile at the question. He had underestimated Brummell. Turning to the crowd, he explained, "Mr. Brummell is right. We found no keys on the corpse, yet his attaché case had clearly been opened to remove Miss Credo's incriminating evidence. She must have taken the keys from the body, but what happened to them afterward? My guess is that you threw it out your window, trusting the snow to conceal their tiny form. Otherwise, why wouldn't you have just put them back on the corpse? No one would have known." Even Robinson turned, expectant, toward the young woman.

"I forgot about them," she replied in a tone disturbingly conversational. "I didn't realize they were still in my pocket until later. It was too late to go back and return them, and I figured it was too risky to simply toss them out the window." She paused, cocking her head slightly to the side while meeting Robinson's gaze. "So I swallowed them." A few gasps filled the room.

Robinson held her eyes for a moment before allowing himself a small smile. "Where did you really put them?"

"Down the toilet. And yes," she replied, raising a hand to ward off further questions, "I know you might well have gotten around to searching wherever the waste goes and eventually found it. But it wouldn't have been traceable to me."

"I salute your professionalism, *madame*, if not the cause you serve. And with that, ladies and gentlemen, our work here is concluded."

The gathering broke up quickly, the passengers gazing

hatefully at Credo as they stood and made their way back to their rooms. Finally, only Robinson, Brummell, and Credo remained along with two porters detailed to guard her. Brummell stood, looked at her wordlessly for several moments, and then turned and silently walked back toward the *Loch Awe.*

With Robinson's permission, the three engines surged forward, horns and whistles blaring as they passed the work crews that had cleared the way. The *National Limited* glided away from the scene of the crime, its passengers left to contemplate a base act of murder while gazing out their windows at a valley of pure, white snow.

CHAPTER FIFTEEN

GRAFTON, WEST VIRGINIA

They stood on the platform, the passengers of the late-arriving *National Limited*, ostensibly to stretch their legs. The snow had stopped and the platform had been cleared, and the large yard in which the station was situated provided a constant clatter of noise and motion as the railroad struggled to make up the many hours lost to the line closure. One could almost sense the anticipation of the mighty steam engines, eager to leap forward with their freights after a long period of boredom. The passengers, for their part, matched this mood with their own palpable excitement; they had really come, not to stroll and stretch, but to see the resolution of the drama that had played out unknowingly in their midst over a late night and lazy morning of snow-related delays.

The police were there in force by the time they had arrived—all four of them, Grafton's finest. Their own nervous energy emerged as they paced or hooked their thumbs, cowboy-like into their gun belts. Spy apprehension was clearly not an everyday element of their work, but more and better law enforcement were said to be on the way; Robinson knew this to be true in part thanks to a telegram he had sent to an old friend in Washington the moment the train had arrived. The reply had come back quickly, promising agents along with the sincere thanks of some very important people. Apparently, Schmitt's network had been a problem for over a year, and the combination of its end and the capture of one of its members was sufficient to put everyone in a good mood. It was at that moment that Robinson had begun to wonder if Credo's prediction of leniency had some merit.

Among the passengers gathered stood James Brummell, freshly cleared of suspicion but exhausted and innervated after the events of the long night. He genuinely appreciated the bracing effect of the cold air as he milled about, separate from the rest of the passengers at the very back of the *Capitol Escort*. Turning to survey the scene, he looked up at the massive B&O station hotel, rising many stories above Grafton's other little buildings, both of the town and of the enormous yard that sat at its heart. The hotel was magnificent, made of brick with ornate stone touches and a fine roof in the Beaux Arts style. Its elegance stood in marked contrast to the hardscrabble, industrial town that it dominated.

James wished he could retire from the scene of this fiasco to a comfortable bed in that hotel, hiding his face from the crowd and the woman and the detective. He had very nearly lost his career and, worse, had very nearly been party to an incident that would have disgraced his department and possibly the Marshall Plan itself. Moments like this, though rare, made him somber and doubtful of himself and the path that he walked.

He sighed to himself as a flick of his finger caused his pocket watch to leap from his breast pocket. As good as the hotel looked, he still had work to do in St. Louis.

And then they appeared. Under the guard of two porters and a conductor, the woman calling herself Miranda Credo stepped down from the *Capitol Escort* onto the platform. Still clad in red, still stunning. If anything, she looked even more glamorous than when she first walked into James's life on that platform the previous day, striding through the iron gates at the last possible minute.

She spared not a glance at the crowd, and instead strode forward confidently—so confidently, in fact, her guards visibly jumped—toward the young man standing apart from the crowd and beside the man in whose charge she was detained, Ellicott Robinson, special inspector of railroad police.

"I see the crowd is out to see the hero," she said to the two men with a hint of warmth in her voice.

"Hero? No, I'm just doing my job," Robinson responded with a hint of false humility.

"No, *me*," Credo corrected. "You know, the one who stabbed the evil Soviet spy to death? The one who put an end to a monstrous web of corruption that endangered the Republic? And all that."

"Absurd," Robinson remarked, though he couldn't keep a trace of a smile out of the corner of his mouth.

"I'm glad you're here, James," Credo continued, turning to the younger man. "I really did enjoy dinner with you, even though you were technically my target."

At a loss for words, the young man muttered a simple thanks.

"For what it's worth, I didn't mean to hurt you. You know, *personally*. I did mean to frame you, but, well…"

"You were doing what you thought you needed to. To survive," he finished for her.

She smiled, a genuine smile of warmth and gratitude. "You understand. Somehow, I thought you would."

"Despite it all," Brummell said, "I hope you…end up OK. You're obviously smart, and you could probably do a lot of good if you cooperate. For yourself, but also for all of us."

"You almost make me a patriot, James. You're infectious. I'm glad I didn't kill you and try to frame Schmitt."

At his unblinking stare, she added, "That was only a backup plan."

"Right," he said, unconvinced.

Suddenly leaning forward, she planted a small kiss on his cheek. "Don't worry about me, charmer of countesses," she said playfully, "I'll have them pinning a medal on me over this before I'm through. You'll see. And then we'll see about having that after dinner drink I was promised *properly*. With only the normal quotient of murder and mayhem."

With that, she turned to her captor. "Take me away, Mr. Robinson. I suppose it was an honor to be caught by a railroad cop of your caliber." She actually sounded gracious, and Brummell wondered just how afraid she had to be under the skin.

"Miss Credo, please come this way," Robinson instructed, guiding her toward the waiting police.

"Wait," Brummell said as they turned away. "Who are you? Your real name?"

Tossing a glance over her shoulder, she smiled briefly and allowed her face to go neutral. Gone was the bluster, the pride, the deception, if only for a moment. "Sarah." And with that, she turned away and was gone.

Brummell watched her go with a mixture of satisfaction and regret. He knew the part he had played in bringing her to justice, and what that might mean for the security of the nation. He also felt used—by her, by Schmitt, and even by Robinson—and wished that the whole bloody mess could have turned out differently.

Having handed off his charge to the police, Robinson turned and walked back toward Brummell. The conductors were beginning to herd the onlookers onto the train, and the engines hooted their readiness to continue the much-delayed journey.

Reaching the diplomat, Robinson considered him before speaking. "She may be right, you know," he said simply.

"I'm not sure how that makes me feel," James responded.

Robinson nodded, "I understand."

The crowds were busy boarding as the train's whistle hurried them along. Sarah was gone, disappeared into a police car.

"I will take this matter in hand until the proper authorities arrive. And, James, I will keep an interest in it even after." He sniffed, averting his eyes slightly. "And I promise that I will let you know how it fares."

James nodded slightly, an earnest if tired expression of appreciation for the gentility of the older man in what was a confusing moment for the younger. Withdrawing a business card from his waistcoat, he offered it to Robinson. The other's hand reached out to receive, opening to reveal his own card already concealed in the palm. The two exchanged the cards wordlessly, each knowing that the affair that had entangled them would not end until the case of Sarah found closure. And each, perhaps, sensing that a mutual respect had elevated them from investigator and chief suspect to something more akin to friendship.

"Thank you, Mr. Robinson, for including me in this. You gave me a chance to help save myself, and that is beyond price."

Robinson offered a slight smile. "I should be thanking you for helping me unravel this charade."

"Ah, but you're not," James replied with a smirk.

Robinson smiled widely, appreciating the banter. "We work well together, James. A pity you waste your talents on high politics. There are mysteries to unravel, property to protect—"

"Dry laws to enforce?"

Both men issued forth weary, breathy laughs.

The train was almost ready, and the conductor up the platform turned his attention to Robinson, awaiting his signal that the train was released to resume its journey.

Extending his hand, Robinson spoke with renewed seriousness. "It has been a pleasure. What we did here mattered, and we will each carry it forward with us."

Taking the proffered hand, James replied, "It has been an *honor.*" They grasped firmly, a single, slow shake. "Until the next journey," James said, releasing and turning back toward the *National Limited.*

"Until then, James," Robinson replied as the other stepped up into the vestibule.

Stepping back from the train, Robinson doffed his Homberg at the conductor. With the word given, his whistle came to his lips and pierced the air. Then came the thunderous roar of the horn of the engine, and the hiss of the breaks, and the clang of the bell. The limited leapt forward, ever chasing its horizon.

Made in the USA
Lexington, KY
01 December 2019